I0617092

An Elegant Swan

By

June E. Bradley

Published by
Melange Books, LLC
White Bear Lake, MN 55110
www.melange-books.com

An Elegant Swan ~ Copyright © 2013 by June Bradley

ISBN: 978-1-61235-702-7 Print

Cover Art by Becca Barnes

An Elegant Swan
June Bradley

An Elegant Swan is a love story set in the time when letter writing was one of the main sources of communication.

Ten years ago, Nancy Smith fell in love with her brother's best friend Lt. Commander Sam Arlington, but their courtship is hindered by her Bipolar sister, Rita and a future senator who thinks Nancy would make the perfect senator's wife. Sam goes out to sea before Nancy learns she is pregnant. With no word from him she gets on with her life.

Chapter One

Smithfield, Virginia, 1965

Lieutenant Commander Sam Arlington looked forward to leaving his duties aboard ship behind. He was spending the weekend with his best friend, Lieutenant Commander Jeremiah Smith, at his family home in Smithfield, Virginia. Jerry was getting married in eight-weeks, and Sam was his best man.

When they arrived at the house and got out of the car, they saw a group of teenagers playing ball in the back yard. Someone yelled, and Sam saw a kid running into the sun trying to catch a fly ball. He didn't move fast enough, and the next thing he knew, he was sprawled on the ground, caught in a tangle of arms and legs.

This definitely wasn't the way to start the weekend. Sam discovered the long arms and legs entwined with his belonged to a girl.

"Damn it. Didn't you see the fly ball coming at you and have enough sense to get out of the way?" her angry voice chided him.

She didn't give him a chance to answer when he tried to move. The softness of her brown hair brushed his face. Rising on her elbows, sharp bones jabbed him, and her lower body pressed into his. A primitive need raced through him. Hazel eyes flecked with gold searched his face. By the expression in her eyes, she knew exactly what was happening between them.

He had seen smoldering passion before, but nothing like this. His heart split like an atom and flared in all directions at once. His feelings skyrocketed. He hadn't experienced anything like this. This girl was making him feel like a randy teenager as ripples of desire snaked through his body. Embarrassed by his wayward thoughts, he tried to move from under her, but her body melded into his.

"Oh," was all she said.

The amused voice of his friend, Jerry brought Sam back to reality as he reached down and pulled the girl off him.

"Sam, meet my kid sister, Nancy."

Sam quickly stood up shaking the grass and dirt from his pants and shirt. It wasn't a boy or a kid, but a girl probably in her late teens or early twenties. Jerry frowned at his sister's disheveled appearance.

"Besides plowing into Sam, did you have to smother him too?"

"Jerry!" The girl smiled and flew into his arms. "We weren't expecting you until tomorrow." Her voice quivered with excitement as she hugged her brother.

"Take it easy, sis." Jerry laughed. "We'll be at the shipyard for the next several months, so they tell us." He slipped out of her embrace.

Sam let out a sigh of relief, glad she wasn't Jerry's bride-to-be. His heart regained its rightful place in his chest. So, this was one of Jerry's sisters. She was a charmer, and he felt as though he already knew her by what Jerry had told him. She attended a local college in Norfolk, was in her senior year, and very smart. Jerry had spoken often about Nancy, but said little about his older sister, Rita. He's said she was bipolar and to be careful of her changing moods. One moment she was happy, and the next moment she was depressed and very jealous of her younger sister.

"Oh, Jerry," Nancy said joyously, and her happiness shown in her smile and bright, shinning eyes.

"It's good to be home. The man you just berated in such glowing terms is Sam Arlington, my friend and best man." Jerry turned his grin toward Sam. "As I said before, this is my kid sister, Nancy."

"I'm not a kid anymore. I'm eighteen and in my last year of college. I'll graduate in June." She glared at her brother in mock anger.

Tall and thin, Nancy came to his shoulder, just right for kissing. What made him think of that? Her worn jeans and a tight fitting tank top showed off her slim figure and small firm breasts. He liked what he saw. She was also taking in everything about him. Yet her appraisal didn't embarrass him. For reasons he didn't understand, he wanted more than just her approval. She was Jerry's kid sister and much too young for him.

The effect of her nearness aroused feelings in him he didn't comprehend.

Their hands met and a flame of sensation ran through him. He clasped her hand longer than he should have, liking the feel of her soft skin against his calloused palm.

"It's nice to meet you, Sam. I hope I didn't hurt you. I go all out when I'm playing ball."

Nancy had an impish grin on her face, and Sam returned her smile. Something was happening between them. He looked directly into her eyes and saw a challenge. He wanted to avoid the feelings already simmering between them. This young lady was dynamite and a charmer. Someday she would break a man's heart, if she already hadn't. He was pretty sure he wasn't ready for that.

Jerry's other sister, Rita, greeted them at the house. She was a delicate and sophisticated blonde version of Nancy.

"Jerry, we were wondering when you'd get home."

"I'm here now," He reached for a hug, and she backed away, holding him at arms length and examining him.

Sam thought it strange Rita didn't take Jerry in her arms like Nancy did, kissing and hugging him after being away so long.

"My goodness, how you've changed," she said with a note of surprise.

"I've been gone over a year, and I'm a man of the world now," he answered in mock bravado.

"So I see." Rita shifted her gaze from Jerry and looked past him to Sam for the first time. She gave Sam an inviting smile. "Jerry, please introduce us."

"Rita, this is my good friend, Sam." Jerry bowed with a flourish to his sister. "He's going to be my best man."

Sam took her hand and felt it tremble as he slowly withdrew his. She was altogether different from Nancy.

"I'm pleased to meet you, Rita," Sam spoke in a self-assured manner.

Rita was all smoothed and polished, with blonde hair and blue eyes that could light up a man's heart or cut him cold. He sensed that coldness. Her appreciative look surprised him. Her appraisal wasn't as obvious as Nancy's had been, but just as direct. She evidently liked what she saw. She was a lady, and expected to be treated like one. Nancy was a rough-cut stone that needed a lot of polishing before she would shine and could compete with her sister.

"Thank you for inviting me. It's not often I have the opportunity to spend a weekend in the country."

"I hope you'll enjoy your stay." Rita's inviting smile oozed with southern hospitality.

* * * *

Nancy leaned against the kitchen counter and watched her sister butter up Sam. Rita would be all over Jerry's friend before the weekend ended. A new man and her sister brightened up like the dawn on a sunny day. That would leave Nancy would little chance of attracting Sam's attention.

Rita, at twenty-six, was using her charms to entice Sam. She left Nancy behind when she used her smile and seductive ways. She would definitely let Nancy know in no uncertain terms that Sam was way out of her league.

Used to it by now, Nancy still cursed. Why shouldn't she have a chance? Once men saw behind Rita's smiling face, selfish moods, and ways, they generally left. Sam looked like he was worth a wait, and Nancy had the time.

She looked at Rita puzzled by her remark to Sam about staying. "Why shouldn't he enjoy his stay?" All eyes turned her way.

Rita stared at her sister with impatience. "It's the polite thing to say when you have guests and want them to feel welcome. Haven't you learned anything I've taught you since mother died?" Her lips drew into a thin, forced smile.

"How could I forget? You keep reminding me," Nancy answered in a sarcastic voice.

Ignoring her younger sister, Rita again turned to Sam. "I hope we can spend some time together. It would be nice to talk to someone new."

"Thank you."

Sam always liked blondes, and this one was a stunner. He wouldn't mind spending some time with her, but there was a problem, her illness. He'd have to be very careful around her. There was more to her request then wanting to talk. Sam liked a lady who knew her mind. Rita was a very attractive woman, more of what an officer's wife should be, but he wasn't looking for a wife or any other kind of relationship.

Sam had loved Dena, his ex-sweetheart, until he received her 'Dear John letter' six months ago, informing him she married someone else. Lucky for him, his ship was on a yearlong cruise around the world, and his work and foreign ports kept him busy. He had little time to think about Dena or her letter.

On the other hand, Nancy was young and exciting and would be a lot of fun to be with. She was on her way to becoming a beauty. What choices. He never realized how different sisters could be because he didn't have any. He caught Nancy watching him and gave her what he thought was a brotherly smile. Yet, earlier this afternoon, he hadn't felt the least bit brotherly toward her.

Jerry noticed the coolness between his sisters and changed the subject. "Where's Dad?"

"He's in the library with Tom," Rita announced.

Sam saw Rita perk up at the mention of her father's guest. Was Tom a close friend? Rita sounded excited, and he wondered if he would be invading Tom's territory if he asked her out?

"Tom arrived while you were out playing ball. You know he comes often to ask Dad's advice, and he's still here." Rita was cool to her sister. "They're huddled in Dad's office discussing strategy for Tom's campaign."

Nancy turned to Sam to explain. "Tom's a family friend running for the State Senate and Dad is helping him with his campaign."

"I don't know why you and Tom don't hit it off," Rita said. "He has a bright future ahead of him, and he'll be an important man someday."

"Right now, Tom is more interested in politics than any woman," Nancy replied.

Sam and Jerry listened to the discussion between the sisters.

"How can you say that?" Rita demanded, coming to Tom's defense. He likes you very much, and he always wants to take you places."

"I keep telling him I'm not interested," Nancy said. "I only want to be friends and politics isn't my cup of tea. You like all the glitz and glamour of politics, and you're better suited for that kind of life. You'd make him a better trophy wife."

"I don't like your remark about being a trophy wife. Tom and I would work together." Rita declared with a saccharin sweet smile.

"Hey, break it up, girls. We have company." Jerry's frown showed he wasn't happy with his sisters bickering in front of Sam.

Rita gave Sam an inviting smile. "See you later." She turned and left the room.

"I'm sorry, Sam," Nancy apologized. "I shouldn't let my irritation with Rita show. She's always on my back about something. No matter what it is, I never measure up."

"I understand. My cousin and I had problems too."

So, Nancy and her sister had these occasional differences of opinion. Evidently, Nancy only wanted to be friends with this Tom person while Rita wanted more. It made for an interesting situation.

Sam and Jerry went down the hall to Jerry's father's office. The door was closed and Jerry knocked.

"Come in," came a strong reply.

Jerry opened the door and entered with Sam and Nancy behind him.

"Jerry!" Mr. Smith got out of his chair and came to greet and embrace his son.

Edward Smith was tall with gray hair. He was a retired Navy Captain and from what Jerry had told Sam, he spent his retirement dabbling in local real estate and was a history buff.

"It's so good to have you home, son."

"I'm glad to be home, Dad." Jerry pulled away from his father. "Dad, this is my good friend and best man, Sam Arlington."

Mr. Smith shook Sam's hand. "It's good to meet you, Sam. I'm glad Jerry has a good friend and brought you home to meet us."

Sam's hand buckled under the strength of the older man's grip, before he released it. "Thank you, sir. It's good to get off the ship for a change after our long cruise."

Nancy gave her father a peck on the cheek and spoke softly to the man standing next to him. "Hi, Tom."

"Hello, darling." His words were possessive and challenging.

Sam saw Nancy wince. He guessed she wasn't happy seeing Tom and have him calling her 'darling.'

"This is Tom Brewster, the son of an old family friend," Jerry's dad said. "Tom is a lawyer and running for the State Senate in the next election. He's one of our town's up and coming politicians."

"It's nice to meet you, Tom." Sam saw the shrewdness in the other man's eyes as they shook hands.

The first thought that came to Sam's mind was what an arrogant bastard this man was. He could see why Nancy wasn't interested in him. He would be right at home in politics.

"It's always nice to meet Jerry's friends when he brings them home. Of course, he can't be around as much as we'd like him to be. Enjoy your stay, Sam. It's nice country here."

"I'm sure I will," Sam replied. Instantly he knew he could never be friends with this man. Tom looked at Sam with an insincere smile on his face while he sized up the competition.

The battle lines for the Smith women's' attentions were drawn. Tom would be in for a surprise when he learned Sam was interested in Rita and not Nancy, or so he thought.

This afternoon's closeness with Nancy had to be some kind of a fluke. Tom looked at Nancy as if she was a chocolate sundae waiting to be devoured. Sam wondered if Tom realized how obvious he was in his feelings for the girl.

A few minutes later, Nancy spoke. "Sorry to break up this family gathering, but I have to leave."

"You're leaving already?" Tom protested.

Nancy turned and smiled at everyone. "I have some homework to finish." She went over, gave her father a hug and a kiss, and left the room.

Tom had the smooth look of a politician wanting to talk, while assessing the fatness of his constituents' wallets and from his expression crossed Sam off his list in every way.

Sam had the feeling Tom didn't like having competition for the Smith women. The look he gave him was more of a warning to stay away from what he considered his. Tom was in for a big surprise. From where Sam stood, he had the choice of two beautiful women. Rita was delicate and eager for his attention while Nancy was holding back. What man could resist such delightful ladies when they were being displayed for his pleasure?

Sam realized Jerry and his father were watching the invisible battle waging between the two men. Their expressions were amused. Jerry knew Sam's interest in politics, but Tom didn't.

Jerry grinned. "Tom, are you finally making a run for the State Senate?"

"Yes, I have the backing I need." He was animated.

"How long will you be in dry dock, son?" Edward said, changing the subject.

"Six to nine months. It depends on the war. Sam and I are both expecting orders."

"I see," a frown crossed Edward's face. He sat down and invited the men to join him.

"It looks like the girls are still disagreeing with each other," Jerry observed.

"It's more like a war zone since Rita returned home. You know how she likes everything to be in perfect order and not a hair out of place, especially if she's in one of her moods," Edward explained. "She was never as easy going as Nancy. They're as opposite as night and day. Nancy is always happy and content no matter what."

That wasn't how Sam had perceived Rita, but he had just met her. It wouldn't be the first time he'd been wrong about a beautiful woman.

"Rita gave Sam a nice warm welcome." Jerry remarked with a hint of amusement.

"Glad to hear that. She isn't too friendly with the new people she meets," Edward replied.

"What happens when you and Ruth decide to marry?" Jerry said.

A thoughtful expression crossed Edward's face. "When we do, we hope Rita will accept Joe Hoskins proposal and marry him. He's been hanging around since she came home. However, you never know with your sister. She's up one day and down the next. Sometimes, if you just look at her crossways, she flies off the handle."

"Joe Hoskins?" Jerry said. "Didn't they go together for a while?"

"Yes, before she met and went away with that guy, Jason who was into all that weird stuff. She thought she was in love with him. It wasn't long before he threw her out. She was in pretty bad shape and was stranded in Boston when we learned of her whereabouts. "

"He must have been a real low life." Jerry said.

"He was. We had to go to Boston and bring her home. Thank goodness, they hadn't married. Bedsides, the drugs he'd been feeding her and her mental state sent her spiraling out of control. She's never gotten over the fact he left her for someone else. We had to put her in a rehab center for awhile to help get her back to a somewhat normal condition," Edward told them.

"She never learns, does she?" Jerry shook his head.

"It's a good thing they weren't married or it would have been one hell of a mess," Edward replied. "Joe's so in love with her, he would do anything for her. He's a contractor and doing well."

Jerry appeared surprised at what his father reported. "Rita should have married Joe."

"Sorry, about this family discussion, Sam," Edward said. "We're glad to have you for the weekend. With Jerry's wedding coming up, maybe we'll see you more often. Anything you want or need, just ask any one of us or Mattie, our housekeeper and cook. She's around most of the time. We're very informal here, so make your self comfortable."

"Thank you, sir." Sam already felt himself relaxing.

"I hope you'll excuse Tom and me for awhile longer. We have some business to finish."

Tom had pretended to be busy, but Sam hadn't missed any of Tom's actions.

Chapter Two

Sam didn't see Nancy again until that evening at dinner. He wasn't the only dinner guest. Tom also stayed for the evening meal. Nancy wore a fancy pair of form fitting jeans and a scooped neck top. Rita ripped into her about her attire before she was able to sit down.

"Go change those clothes immediately." Rita's face appeared white with anger.

"There's nothing wrong with my clothes," Nancy snapped back.

"No decent girl would wear anything like that on a date, unless she was looking for trouble."

"I think she looks very nice," Tom said. He didn't seem to mind being in the middle of the sister's disagreement. He'd evidently been there many times.

"You would," Rita sneered, ignoring Tom's intervention. "Nancy, go change those clothes, now."

"The clothes your sister has on are what all the college girls are wearing." Edward's irritation at his oldest daughter demand was obvious.

Rita stood up, glaring at Nancy. "You look like a tramp."

Their father's voice sounded loud and clear. "Rita, please sit down and apologize to your sister or leave the table."

Rita, in a huff, threw her napkin down, moved out from the table, and left the room without saying another word.

"I'm sorry, Dad. I didn't think she would get in such a tizzy. She never seems to be satisfied with anything I do."

Sam thought Nancy looked cute in her outfit. It emphasized her figure. Her pants were form fitting, but not skin tight. They seemed to hug every curve of her young body and had Sam's imagination working overtime. He told himself to knock it off. She was only eighteen. She was of age, barely, but she was also his friend's younger sister. So he needed to keep his thoughts elsewhere.

Jerry excused himself and a few minutes later brought Rita back to the table. She stared at Nancy and, even though she didn't look repentant, apologized.

"I accept your apology," Nancy said.

Nothing else was said about the incident, and everyone continued on with their meal and conversation. Several times Sam caught Tom watching him and Nancy when he thought no one was watching. If Tom figured he could make points with Nancy by taking her side, it wasn't working. She was polite when he talked to her, but she didn't go out of her way to carry on a conversation with him.

Did Nancy know how appealing she was? Did she have the same effect on other men as she did on him and Tom? Sam's reactions to the each sister were totally different. Rita was slim, glamorous, somewhat reserved, and would look good on a man's arm. Nancy was young and exuberant, but would eventually become a stunning beauty. He kept telling himself she was too young, but something about her kept drawing him to her. He tried to keep his mind on the dinner conversation and found it hopeless.

Sam's eyes strayed from sister to sister. At times, Nancy exchanged glances with him, and he found himself floundering in her golden green eyes. Her eyes reminded him of calming seas at sunset.

Rita watched them with a look he couldn't fathom. She didn't approve of Nancy, and it left him curious. Jerry had warned him about Rita. She had just gone through a nasty relationship and had not gotten over it. High strung all her life according to Jerry, Rita was jealous of her sister and brother. Tom's eyes narrowed when he saw the way Nancy looked at Sam.

The front door bell rang. Nancy excused herself and went to answer it. She seemed eager and evidently was expecting someone. Nancy returned with a young man and introduced him.

"Billy, you know everybody but my brother's friend, Sam. He's going to be best man at Jerry's wedding."

"Billy Walker, this is Sam Arlington."

Sam stood and the two shook hands in a cool, polite manner. Sam watched Billy eye Nancy and decided he was another candidate for her affections.

Before Nancy left, she kissed each of her family, including Tom and Sam on the cheek. It was obvious Rita wasn't pleased with her sister's actions. Then there was Tom, he missed nothing of what was going on. After the meal was finished, everyone retired to the living room.

* * * *

Afterwards, when Tom was leaving, Rita saw him to the door.

"It was so nice having you for dinner, Tom. I wish you could stay longer." She cooed.

"Thanks for having me. Tom was about to go out the door, when Rita leaned over and kissed him, rubbing her body against his in an intimate way. He gently pushed her away.

"Rita, behave yourself." He said quietly, but everyone could hear.

"You shouldn't be wasting your time on Nancy," Rita said. "You know she isn't right for you

Tom smiled. "And you are?"

"Of course, I am. It will take Nancy years to become polished and presentable. I'm the type of woman you need." Rita moved closer to him.

"We've had this talk before, Rita. First, you're not my type, and second, I can't afford a wife with your condition." His impatience showed.

"So, I have a little depression that shows up once in a while."

"That's the point. We could be at an affair and, if you had one of your seizures, it could be very embarrassing for me. I don't need that. There's no telling how you would react or what you would do to me and my guests."

"I'm much better suited to you, and I have the glamour and polish you need for your way of life."

"You may think so, but we've been through this many times. The answer is still no."

"You've made it clear it's Nancy you want. I'm afraid you've got new competition, and I don't think you'll win." She pushed Tom out the door and slammed it behind him.

* * * *

Rita didn't rejoin them in the living room.

"Sam," Edward said, "I'm sorry you had to witness Rita's behavior. It's embarrassing to all of us, but it doesn't seem to bother her at all. She's always had a thing for Tom. She thought dating someone else would make him jealous and, when it didn't work, she ran off with Jason. It wasn't what she expected and only made things worse. She's always reaching for the glamour and the glitz. When she finds it isn't what it should be, she nosedives into depression."

"I understand, sir. Jerry told me about her problem."

Jerry had given him the bare facts about Rita, and it was good of his father to explain her illness. They also discussed the situation in Vietnam, the Navy, and how long they expected their ship to stay in Norfolk. After awhile, Sam excused himself and left Jerry to spend time with his father.

Jerry had shown Sam to his room earlier, and he had dropped off his overnight bag and looked forward to the nice inviting bed instead of a ship bed. On the way to his room, Rita waylaid him at the bottom of the stairs. She appeared in a better frame of mind now that Nancy wasn't around and she had his sole attention. She was more animated' than she had been earlier in the evening.

"Would you like to join me in a nightcap?"

Her mood was inviting, and she grabbed his hand to pull him into a small room off the hallway. He could feel her hand shaking.

"Sure, why not?" Sam really didn't want to be with her, but thought it would be impolite to refuse. Rita might give him some information about Nancy, but considering what happened earlier in the evening she might not. Then again, why was he interested in a college kid, when he had a beautiful woman inviting him to join her for a drink?

Rita moved closer to him, oozing charm and sexuality. She was tipsy, and the smell of whisky was noticeable.

"Do you plan on making the Navy your career," Her words slurred as she spoke. Rita's self-confidence had returned after Tom's rejection.

"Yes, I hope to make Captain some day."

"Just like my father. That's a lofty goal. Her smile gave way to disappointment.

"It can be accomplished with determination and the right mindset," he said.

"You will." She smiled at him.

"Yes." He nodded. "Your father was in for thirty years and retired as a Captain, but it doesn't sound as if you like military life.

"No, I don't." She spoke with heat.

"I'm making it my career," he said just as empathically.

"I wish you luck." She appeared disappointed in his answers. Her smile was a poor imitation of one of Nancy's.

"Thank you." He wasn't sure she meant what she said.

Rita moved closer, and he could see the overly bright sparkle in her blue eyes. He felt the urge to leave. She took his arm and moved closer to him. Her fragrance, elusive yet tantalizing, didn't cover up the smell of liquor on her breath. Still, he floundered in her nearness.

His arms went around her. Their lips met. Her mouth and her body devoured him. She was all over him. If she got any closer, she'd be at his backside.

That's what a beautiful woman and a year at sea did to a man. She moved out of his arms as quickly as she moved into them, and a great sense of relief washed over him. The whiskey smell on her breath was overpowering.

"What would you like to drink, Sam.?"

"A ginger ale with ice would be fine."

If she's on medication, she shouldn't be drinking liquor. Where did she get it? If there was some in the house, Sam was sure her father hid it or had it under lock and key. Sam wasn't going to let her actions and eagerness blur his senses. Once was enough. She was moving too fast for him.

"Oh, come on, Sam, a big man like you can handle a drink stronger than ginger ale." An inviting smile crossed her face.

"I'm not a drinking man," he said.

"You've got to be kidding." She looked at him in surprise. "You're a sailor.

"I've seen too many careers ruined because the men drank too much."

"In that case, ginger ale it is. I'm going to have Scotch on the rocks. It soothes one's nerves."

"Are you nervous about something?"

"No more than usual," she said with an airy wave of her glass.

While Rita fixed her drink, Sam made himself comfortable on the couch. Even in the dim light, he saw her hands shake and the mixer rattle against the glass. He wondered how much she had had to drink before she waylaid him. The smell of liquor was overwhelming. He had to turn sideways to keep from coughing. Jerry had told him about his sister and he changeable moods. He had forgotten that part. Now he knew he had to get away from her as quickly and smoothly as possible.

She settled on the couch next to him and deliberately spilled her drink on his jeans. He started to get up, but she held him down.

"Here, let me take care of that."

She reached across his body for a napkin and let her breasts rub against him. He found himself in a dilemma. She was his friend's sister, but with her brazen ways, finding a way to leave and not embarrass either of them presented a challenge.

"I'm generally not this clumsy," Rita purred.

"It's quite all right." He reached over and took the napkin from her hand. He stood up, wiped off his damp jeans, and then put the napkin down. When he straightened up, she was standing too close to him.

She raised her hand to bring his face down to hers and gave him a French kiss. Then, with a mischievous smile, she quickly moved away from him, her eyes glowing in the half-light.

"Good night and sweet dreams." She turned majestically and walked out of the room like a reigning queen.

Sam stood in a mystified daze. He was surprised by all the changes he experienced with this woman. All of them had been smoothly calculated, and he had fallen into her trap. He had been outmaneuvered in more ways than one. Thankfully, nothing had happened.

* * * *

Sam undressed in the darkness of the guest bedroom thinking about Jerry and his sisters. Rita certainly was unpredictable. The moves she made on him had been smooth, wanton, and deliberate. Was she really interested in him or just flirting because he was someone different or was it because Rita thought Nancy might be interested in him? He'd met two pretty women in one day who affected him in different ways.

Rita knew what she wanted and went after it. Then what? Could she follow through or was it just a flirtatious game to her? Did she think this was the beginning of a serious relationship after one meeting? If she was looking for a serious relationship, she was looking in the wrong place. She was fragile and not his type. She had already told him, she didn't like military life. He was still getting over Dena's rejection and had no intentions of starting a new relationship just now.

The woman who would share his life had to be strong and face the rigors of being a Navy wife. She had to be prepared for many unseen challenges. There were unexpected changes in orders. He could ship out at any time. Ships were often diverted to answer SOS calls and could meet unexpected delays. The looming war threatened more uncertainties. Right now, he was only looking for companionship, nothing more.

Rita seemed to have all the qualifications to make an officer's wife, but could she stay the course? According to Tom, she couldn't. On this, he agreed with Tom, especially after her actions this evening. What had caused her affair to end? It had to be something other than her sickness. What the hell was he thinking? There was no way he could attach himself to a woman as unpredictable as Rita.

Then there was Nancy, a young woman full of spirit. She was still a college kid and twelve years younger than he was. When the time came, she would meet life head on. Those erotic feelings he had when their bodies touched had to be a fluke. How could heat and passion build up so fast between two people who had just met?

Rita complained about her kid sister, but she was more wanton then Nancy. He could see the grace and elegance in Nancy's walk and manner that would come when she got older. She wasn't ready to surrender her independence and her heart. The man she gave them to would have to be someone special, someone she loved deeply and with all her heart, and deep inside he wanted to be that man.

An Elegant Swan

Her long neck and cap of dark hair reminded him of the elegant swans he saw on the lakes of Europe. He thought of her as his 'Elegant Swan.' He was indulging himself when he referred to her as his. There was no chance of them getting together. Besides, he couldn't let it happen. She was of age, but still too young and Jerry's younger sister.

When they collided in the backyard, he had responded all too quickly to Nancy's lithe body. A year at sea was too long for any man. He smiled as he remembered her surprised expression. The thought of her in his arms and her passion ran through his body. It made him quiver with excitement. They hadn't known each other more than a few hours, and he wanted her. Damn it, he wanted her, not her sister.

It was utterly ridiculous so he pushed those thoughts aside. Here he was hankering over a young woman. He was old enough to know better. Treat her like the kid sister he'd never had. He didn't know too much about young women that age, but he would learn, even if it might be difficult. The most important thing was to avoid her as much as possible.

If he gave Rita more attention, maybe his unwanted feelings for Nancy would fade away. However, he was going to behave himself. He couldn't deny he was attracted to both sisters. Nancy was giving Rita a run for her money.

Jerry was a good friend, and their friendship was important to him. His intentions toward Jerry's sisters had to be honorable and above board. Sam tossed and turned in the darkness until he heard a car pull into the drive. Was that the reason he was so restless? Was he waiting for Nancy to come home? He got up and stood by the darkened window, looking out.

He watched Billy walk her to the front door. Her voice was low and they seemed to be arguing. He couldn't make out what they were saying. He was eavesdropping and quickly pulled back, scolding himself for his ungentlemanly behavior. Moments later, Sam smiled when he heard the front door open and close. Why should the fact Nancy didn't linger, please him?

He went back to bed. Sleep and unwanted dreams overtook him, as he tossed and turned with his thoughts bobbing between two attractive and very attentive women.

* * * *

Nancy knew why she hadn't enjoyed her date with Billy tonight. She compared Billy with Sam, and they weren't in the same league. Even though she had just met Sam, she wanted to learn more about him. What would it be like to be in his arms and come alive again, like she did this afternoon? His accidental closeness awakened a passion within her that had lain dormant until now. She liked the feelings he aroused.

Her brother Jerry was at the table in the kitchen with a bottle of beer, some cheese, crackers, and a book. He checked his watch, surprised at seeing her.

"What are you doing home so early?"

"I wasn't having a good time." Nancy pulled up a chair and sat down across from him.

"Why not? From what I heard, you and Billy were pretty tight."

"Not anymore. We had a fight." She didn't smile.

"Oh?"

Was Jerry's just curious or was he interested. It was all he said.

"Do I have to give you a reason?" She sighed.

"No, but I gather this unhappiness with Billy has something to do with Sam's presence, and then there's Tom patiently waiting on the sidelines. He's willing to accept any crumbs you have to offer. He'd like to claim you as his own."

"Don't I know it. Tom is more like a brother than a suitor. No sparks fly when we're together."

"Give the guy a break." Jerry grinned.

"Hey! Whose side are you on?" She spoke with mock indignation.

"Rita thinks Tom's cool and would like to have him for herself."

"She's always had a thing for Tom and would do anything for him. He's a man with a bright future and has all the glitz and glamour Rita craves. Her instability doesn't fit with his plans." She emphasized the last words. "They'd make a good pair if she was trustworthy and dependable. She has tried everything to make him look her way."

"So I noticed with her behavior tonight."

"They used to go out when she was younger and they were much closer. I wish he would show her some affection and ask her out. She's closer to his age than I am. I think something happened between them a long time ago, and he's afraid of what she might say and do."

"Do you have any idea what it could be?" Jerry had a puzzled look on his face."

"I think I do, but I'm keeping it to myself for now."

"The answer is probably locked away in one of those diaries Mom talked you into keeping. Do you still have them?"

"Yes, I do, and they're locked away in a safe place."

"I can imagine what secrets are hidden in them."

"You needn't worry. It's mostly all girl stuff."

"That's nice to know you won't be blabbing any of my mischievous adventures of the past to Sarah."

Nancy ignored that. "Tom and Rita are closer in age and like the same things. She'd be an asset to him and would make him look good. Every politician likes to have a lovely, sexy looking wife on his arm to make his opponents jealous, if nothing else."

"What do you mean by, if only, besides her sickness?"

"She's unpredictable and a perfectionist. She can't tolerate other people's inadequacies. Even though she may be behaving herself, she could slip into one of her moods if she thought she wasn't getting enough attention and could raise hell at any social affair they attended. It wouldn't sit right with his fellow constituents."

"Rita has been that way all her life," Jerry agreed.

"We're used to her. Being a politician's girlfriend and then his wife would be the kind of life she's always wanted. She'd like meeting all those important people, going to parties, and traveling. She would lord it over her friends and be self-important to her hearts content. However, people would soon tire of her turbulent moods. I don't think she can take people shunning her, and they will. Tom is self centered, and I don't think she can stay the course."

"Why are you telling me this?"

"Because her health problems have grown worse, and you need to know and be watchful."

"You've given me a good idea of what to expect from her." Jerry looked thoughtful.

"It would take all night for me to tell you about some of the tricks she's played, looking for attention."

"You two still don't get along. She was very upset with you at dinner."

"She's always upset with me," Nancy said in frustration. "No matter what I do, it's never good enough. I gave up trying to please her. She thinks Dad favors me over her."

"Dad has never played favorites," Jerry said.

Nancy got up from the table and took a glass from the cupboard and a coke from the fridge before sitting down again. She poured the coke into the glass and took a swallow.

"Jason's dumping her hit her hard. She has her high moments, but when she's down and in a depressed mood, she's suicidal and not fit to live with. Daddy keeps the liquor under lock and key, but she still seems to find a way of getting some. Her last attempt at looking for sympathy drove Dad and me up the wall. He took all the liquor and dumped it down the sink. Rita acted as though he was killing her, and she went in a dozy of a slump. We had to put her in the sanitarium for a few months."

"The animosity between the two of you tonight was pretty bad."

"At times, it's worse. You've never been around when the depression really takes over and she's in a down spiral. We've all gone out of our way to help her, but she doesn't want anyone's help."

"Is she still seeing Doctor Rayburn?"

"When Dad suggested it might be a good idea to see him regularly, she hit the roof. She insisted she isn't sick, doesn't need any help, and that we're harassing her. We also had rotten nerve for even suggesting such a thing. I've learned not to give her any kind of advice. My head gets chopped off when I do."

"I see." Jerry's' frown was worrisome.

"Tonight's action at the dinner table was one example of what we go through," Nancy said.

Jerry sighed. "I know I shouldn't feel this way, but I'm glad I haven't been home to witness her outbursts and unhappiness."

"You're lucky. Since the jerk left her, she's been hell to live with."

"Go easy on her. She must be still hurting."

"It's been over a year since it happened. You'd think by now she'd get over it and get on with her life." At the moment, Nancy was feeling less than kindly toward her sister.

"What's this about her and Joe Hoskins?"

"Joe owns his own construction business. He's crazy about her, but you know what a snob Rita can be. As far as she's concerned, he's only a carpenter, and she only keeps him around because there's been no one better in sight until now."

"You mean Sam. Why should she be interested in him? He's a Lieutenant Commander, and she hates the Navy."

"But, she doesn't see him only as a Lieutenant Commander. Instead of two and half gold stripes, she sees four gold stripes. Even though, she claims not to like Navy life, she relishes the prospect of becoming a Captain wife. It's the glamour and prestige she thinks comes with being a high-ranking officer's wife. She should know better.

"We all know it's damn hard work from what Dad and Mom went through when he was in the service."

"She doesn't see it that way. She wants everything now not later. I don't think she'll change her mind about marrying a military man. She's too fragile for all the ups and downs that come with it. The good thing for Mom and Dad was that Mom didn't mind the rigor of Navy life because she loved Dad enough. To her, there was no sacrifice."

"They took good care of us and saw we were well adjusted to every move we made," Jerry said.

"Rita has high expectations, but she lives in a dream world. When something doesn't happen the way she thinks it should, she takes a nosedive, and we all pay for it. Just wait and see." Despite loving her sister, Nancy knew her pretty well. There were times when Rita's crazy behavior left her thoroughly exhausted.

"She has always been impressed by the rich and famous," Nancy said. "Growing up, she vowed she would be one of them. Along the way, reality crept in and brought her down with a huge thud. Her head is still in the clouds and she hasn't given up reaching for the brass ring,"

"How well I remember. When we were kids and played, she always had to be the Queen and you and I her humble servants." Jerry smiled at the memory.

"To Rita, Joe is just a lowly carpenter while he is rich, sober, and reliable. He would build her a house fit for a queen and has loved her since high school. What else could a woman ask for? He makes her laugh and has been around long enough to understand her and her illness.

Even a good man can take just so much."

"Rita has always been different. If only she'd relax and bend a little," Jerry said.

"She won't. You know how she feels about me. I don't come up to her standard for being a lady, and I'm irresponsible, just like our mother. Mom wasn't irresponsible and made Dad happy. They had a long and wonderful life together until she became ill. She still saw we were cared for, and Dad arranged it so he could be with us through the rough times until she died." Nancy remembered their mother with love and affection.

Lost in memories, the two fell silent for a moment.

"Tell me about your friend, Sam?" Nancy watched her brother's expression change to a quiet, thoughtful one.

"What do you want to know?" he said at last.

"All there is to know." She tried not to sound too eager.

"So you're interested in Sam, too? He's a good friend, and we get along fine."

"Damn it! That's not what I mean and you know it." Nancy scowled at her brother.

"I know exactly what you mean," his voice softened. "He's a very popular guy, the love-them-and-leave-them type."

"Ooh." Nancy's heart slid down her insides, leaving a feeling of emptiness.

"You'd gone out with Billy and weren't around to see what happened later. I was passing by the small room off the hall when I saw Rita using her dazzling charms on Sam. She definitely has her eye on him."

"She always has her eye on any new man," Nancy responded.

"Why would you be interested in him? He's much older than you."

She smiled at her brother. "I have a tendency to like older men."

"That may be, but you're still too young for him."

"No I'm not." She gave her brother a big smile. "Did Rita seem overly animated and cheerful tonight?"

"Yes, she was. I thought it might be because she cornered Sam in the den. I saw them, but I didn't interrupt, I was curious to see how Sam handled her. She moved right in on him like a steamroller. He didn't have a chance. Sam came out a little overwhelmed. I'm sure the feeling won't last. He's a pretty savvy guy."

"She's drinking again and mixing it with her medications."

Jerry looked glum. "That's not good even in a normal person. I've been gone a long time. She has definitely changed. So tell me the rest of what's been happening?"

"You're lucky you weren't here to witness Rita's bouts with the bottle and her pills. When she mixes the two of them together, it makes tough going for everyone around here. Dad stopped keeping liquor in the house. He was never much of a drinker, and he only had it for company. I can't drink, because I get a stomachache, not a headache, so I leave it alone. She still gets it from somewhere. There are weeks and days where she's fine, and then some little thing sets her off. She hits a downswing and it really gets rough."

"She seemed all right tonight." Jerry observed.

"Oh yes, she puts up a good front, especially in front of a new man."

"Sam's not that easy to fool, and I warned him about her. He likes his women to be independent and not the clinging vine type."

"Tell me more about Sam."

"Well, his girl friend got tired of waiting, broke off their engagement, and married someone else. He says he's a confirmed bachelor and seems happy the way he is. He doesn't want any complications and tells the ladies before hand he's not interested in a meaningful, long-term relationship. He's happy single and doesn't need any college siren vamping him." He emphasized the last sentence with a big smile."

"Is that what you think I am?" Nancy was disappointed in her brother's remark.

"It's just an expression, and you know me better than that. You haven't had much experience with men like Sam. I don't want to see you get hurt, not that I think he would hurt you. Sam's a great guy, but right now, he's not interested in marriage. You're too young and tempting even for a confirmed bachelor like Sam."

How many times had she been told she was too young for this or that? Her heart dropped to her toes. She'd already lost her heart to Sam. He woke feelings deep inside her when he held her. She never wanted anyone the way she wanted Sam. How could this happen in so short a time?

Belatedly, Nancy responded her brother's question. "Don't I always behave myself?"

"You do most of the time. Don't fall for Sam. You could get your heart broken."

"It's too late," she replied with sadness.

"I had a feeling it might be. I've been away too long and haven't been around to teach you the ways of men like Sam. I forgot that you've grown up and would be interested in the opposite sex. I didn't expect both of you to like him. Just take it slow and easy, baby. If it's to be, it will be, as Mom used to say."

Jerry got up from the table, came over, and took her in his arms. "I happen to love you very much and don't want to see you get hurt."

"I can't promise you anything," she whispered.

Chapter Three

Jerry and Sam stayed weekends at the farm and made life more exciting for Nancy. As she got to know Sam, her feelings for him grew stronger. No man had ever affected like this.

While Sam only saw her as a kid, his actions toward her were friendly and affectionate. He never encouraged their friendship to be more intimate. Yet she always caught him watching her. He was someone new and different from the guys she dated, or was it his uniform? She didn't think so because she had been around uniforms all her life. There was more to it, and it was something she couldn't explain, even to herself. The man intrigued her.

Sam appeared more interested in Rita, but not overly so. She couldn't blame him because they had a lot in common. Rita was twenty-eight, and Sam was two years older.

Nancy worked hard to make Sam see her as a young woman and knew he was fighting the chemistry that sizzled between them. Did he think she was only attracted to him because she was a tomboy and too young for him? She would behave herself and act more feminine and mature. She was willing to give it a damn good try and hoped his feelings would develop into something more than a brotherly interest. Falling in love with Sam wasn't hard to do. It hurt when the man she loved didn't even know she was alive.

Rita and Sam appeared to enjoy each other's company. Nancy wished she knew what Sam was thinking. Her feelings for him were real. If he didn't return them, she would end up with a broken heart. It would be hard to pick up the pieces and move on, but she would.

When Sam came to visit, Nancy stayed out of the way. Her sister didn't like competition. The more Nancy saw of Sam, the harder it was for her to pretend she didn't care, especially when her heart developed a mind of its own. When was Sam going to wake up to the fact Rita wasn't the woman for him?

Nancy had to restrain herself not to compete for his attention. She stayed away from the house as much as she could and returned only after she knew he had left. It made the situation easier and yet her heart ached for his touch.

* * * *

Tom won a vacant seat in the State Senate. He invited them all to a dinner-dance at the Bay Oaks Country Club. At the club, Tom was greeted by well-wishers and friends. Nancy, Jerry, and Sarah, his fiancé, followed the waiter to their table. Sam and Rita arrived late. Rita made her usual grand entrance. Sam seated Rita in a chair facing away from the crowd.

"Sorry we're late." Sam apologized to the group.

"I don't want to sit here," Rita insisted in a petulant voice. "People can't see me. I want your seat, Nancy."

Nancy knew what Rita was up to. She wanted to show off a handsome man like Sam. She wanted to be the center of attention and be admired for her flawless beauty. Nancy wasn't going to argue and spoil everyone's evening. Her sister would do it soon enough. Rita's eyes were glassy. She was high and must have mixed her pills with alcohol, again.

Tom was in a jovial mood. Once the seating was settled, Tom and Nancy danced. The other couples also joined them. It was pure agony for Nancy to see the way Rita clung to Sam.

"Sam seems to like your sister." Tom spoke above the music.

"Yes, they get along well," she replied. She didn't want to sound envious and let Tom see her true feelings for Sam, but somehow he did.

"If you think Sam might be interested in you, forget it. You're too young for a man of his experience." A mocking smile covered his face.

"Then, why are you so interested in me? I'm much younger and don't have the experience and sophistication of Rita."

"Nancy, I've known you all your life, and I know how your mind works. You're smart and pretty. With the right clothes and my knowledge, I could make you into the perfect Senator's wife."

"That's if I said yes and want what you want, but, I don't."

"All you have to do is accept my proposal."

"There's nothing I dislike more than a conceited jackass, and you're definitely one."

Tom laughed, shrugged his shoulders, and smiled knowingly. "Being conceited helps in being a politician."

"What about love?" She spoke in a serious manner.

"I think being compatible and knowing what each one wants from the other person is much better then being in love."

"Oh and why is that?" She'd never been able to understand Tom's way of thinking.

"You lay out the ground rules beforehand. Each person knows exactly what is expected of them and where they stand."

"In other words, it's a legal document like a prenuptial agreement," Nancy said."

"Why not? That way everything is understood. There are no quarrels over money and property if the couple decides to split, and there are no hard feelings."

"Why do choose me and not Rita? She's more your age and meets all of your qualifications."

"She isn't in the running, and you know why. Your sister isn't dependable when the going gets tough. I need a helpmate not a hindrance."

"What makes you an expert on my sister?" Although he wasn't telling her anything she didn't already know, she didn't like the way he talked about Rita. "She is my sister, and I love her."

"I know you do. I've known a lot of women like Rita. She's never satisfied with what she has and is always looking for something new and different."

"You want me, but, you don't think I'm old enough and smart enough to hold on to a man like Sam," Nancy snapped.

"No, I don't." His dislike for Sam was evident, and he wasn't trying to hide it.

"Yet, you think I'd make a good wife for you?"

"With your looks and brains and my knowledge along with the right connections, you'd be the perfect wife."

"It would be fine if I aspired to being the perfect wife, but I'm not interested in doing that."

The impulse to slap the smug look off of his face was uppermost in her mind. She stifled it. She had all she could take of his superior attitude.

"I'd like to sit down." The music was coming to an end.

She knew Rita favored Tom. He would be an important man some day. People in high office and all the glamour and glitz impressed her. She didn't think about all the hard work it took.

Nancy wasn't going to give into Tom's pressure. She knew what she wanted and it wasn't him. She would wait and be patient. They returned to the table, but before they could sit down, Sam turned to her.

"Nancy, do you know how to tango?" He smiled with a twinkle in his eye.

"Yes, I do, and I'd love too," she replied.

Sam took her hand and led her to the dance floor, Tom's face turned sullen. Her sister's jealous look was in full bloom. Damn it! She wanted to dance with Sam. From what she'd seen, he was a good dancer.

Nancy would be in his arms for a few minutes, and she'd be in heaven. He couldn't help but hold her close, making her heart flutter. He led her through the intricate steps with grace and smoothness as though they had danced together for years. There was no time for conversation, and his closeness brought a frisson of heat. When she looked into his eyes, she saw an unmistakable yearning. It quickly disappeared when the dance was over, and he returned her to her seat.

Rita was fuming. Nancy ignored her sister's nasty look and let the unseen daggers of envy glance off her.

"Do you always dance with such vulgarity? Dancing so close to Sam like you wanted to get inside his skin?" Rita's loud words cut the air. Her uncalled for outburst startled everyone, and they stared in disbelief.

Nancy sat devastated and embarrassed by her sister's accusations. The implication caught her off balance.

Sam saw what was happening. "The tango is a beautiful and sensual dance. It's known all over the world for its grace and fluid motion. I enjoyed dancing with you, Nancy. Thank you." He turned so no one else saw him wink at her.

Surprise overtook her and kept her from confronting her sister. Rita was still fuming and had spoiled the evening. Nancy wanted only to leave.

She turned to Tom. "Please take me home." Her voice hardly rose above a whisper.

Tom nodded. He too knew better than to argue with Rita, especially when she had that thunderous look in her eyes.

"I hope you don't mind if Nancy and I leave. I've taken care of the bill."

"Tom, you don't have to do that," Jerry objected.

"It's my pleasure. Good night, everyone." He put Nancy's shawl around her shoulders and pulled her close as they left the room.

* * * *

Jerry watched Tom and Nancy leave. "I think it's time we all left." Sam agreed.

"I don't want to leave, I want to stay." Rita's pout contorted into a mean expression. "I want another drink. After all, it isn't that late."

Embarrassed, Jerry and Sam looked at each other. Jerry wished he could do something about his sister. Whatever he said to her would end up with everyone in the room listening and further embarrass all of them. He wasn't used to her outbreaks anymore. He wanted to shut her up. The rest of the goodnights were civil and polite. Sam and Rita were left alone.

* * * *

On the way home, Nancy was in no mood to talk.

"I'm sorry the evening had to end this way," Tom said.

"I am too, I was enjoying myself." She pulled her shawl closer around her shoulders.

"You and Sam dance well together. It was … well, very provocative. Where did you learn to tango?"

"At school, it's one of my electives. I like it. You can lose yourself in the intricate steps and flow of the music."

"Rita's jealous of you."

"She has no reason to be." Nancy looked at him in the dim light of the car.

"She's using Sam," Tom observed.

"We both know it. She's always having high hopes. A Senator has more prestige than a Lieutenant Commander. It will take years for Sam to become an officer high enough to meet her goals. He would go through hell if he married her."

"We both know that. Your sister likes the glamour associated with being a politician's wife. She sees nothing of the traveling, working long days, and the late hours. She's impatient and wants everything now. It doesn't work that way. I'm not in love with Rita."

"I know, and it annoys the hell out of her. It upsets her that you prefer me to her, and you're not in love with me either. Why do the people we love, love someone else?

"Are you in love with Sam?"

"Yes. I'm sorry, Tom. It's just the way it is."

"I know, but I can still hope. Just be careful." Tom parked in the driveway and reached over and to give her a brotherly kiss on the cheek. She got out of the car.

"Be careful," he said in warning. "Rita's had more than a few drinks tonight. She'll be in a belligerent mood when she comes home."

"Don't worry, I can handle her. She'll be sweet as molasses to Sam and take her unhappiness out on me. I'm used to her moods, but I'm also getting tired of being her scapegoat."

Chapter Four

Tired and frazzled after the scene with Rita at the club, Nancy decided a hot shower would sooth her nerves. Finished, she dried herself, slipped on her robe, and walked into her bedroom and then stopped.

"Oh, my Lord!"

Her room looked like a cyclone had hit it. The clothes in her closet had been pulled off their hangars and lay in a pile on the floor. Rita was now pulling her underwear out of the drawers and throwing it everywhere.

Next, Rita attacked Nancy's bed and pulled the bedcovers off, throwing them on the floor. She overturned furniture and pulled out drawers. All the rest of Nancy's clothes were strewn about the room. Hatred etched her sister's face.

Furious, Nancy knew she could do nothing until Rita's frenzy abated. Just as fast as Rita's fury had escalated, it would wind to a staggering halt. She collapsed against a wall, sliding to the floor and sobbing.

With anger contorting her face, she glared at her younger sister. "You want Sam don't you?" she said in an almost too quiet voice.

"I'm in love with him," Nancy replied. She learned long ago it was better telling her sister the truth than lying.

"Eighteen and in love, puppy love, that's what it is," Rita taunted. "If Sam loved you, it wouldn't last. You couldn't hold on to a man like him."

"Tom told me the same thing. He also said you couldn't stay the course if you married Sam."

"What does Tom know? Sam's going places, and I intend to go with him," Rita insisted.

"You hate Navy life."

"I do, but I can persuade Sam to think my way and see being a civilian is much better. There are more opportunities for him."

"What makes you think he'll give up a career he loves? Has he said anything to you in that direction?" Nancy already knew the answer. Rita was fantasizing again and would ignore her questions.

"He needs a mature and glamorous woman like me. Not some scrawny kid hanging on his arm."

"You think you fit the bill?" Nancy spoke with a quiet calmness.

"Of course, you'd never be able to tame a tiger like Sam," Rita sneered at her sister.

"I'll never know until I try, will I? You went after him because you thought I was interested. It's just like you do with all my boyfriends, and when you get the brush off, you're highly insulted," Nancy observed.

"Sam's new and different." A sob escaped Rita. "Just because you think you're in love with him doesn't mean a thing." Rita got up and then sat on Nancy's disheveled bed, pulling her legs up and resting her elbows on her knees.

"Why do you always feel you have to compete with me? You're prettier and smarter than I am." Nancy knew Rita liked to be flattered.

It wasn't the answer Rita expected. Filled with remorse, she sobbed softly.

Nancy's height enabled her to sit next to her sister and pull her into her arms. She cradled and rocked her like the scared child she was. Nancy released her when her crying subsided. She bent over and put her arms around Rita's waist and lifted her to a standing position.

"I'm sorry," Rita said. She was like a small child, who always needed attention.

"I know you are."

She was always sorry after one of her mood swings. "I want to go to bed." It hadn't taken her long to get back to her demanding ways and to her old self again.

"I'll help you." Nancy sighed, knowing it would be awhile before her sister slept.

She led Rita to her room and turned on the lights. Rita sat on the edge of her bed, and Nancy helped her undress and get into her baby doll pajamas. She didn't want to endanger the fragility of the moment by saying anything that might start her sister off again. Nancy managed to get her into bed and turn out the lights.

"Don't leave me. I don't want to be alone," Rita's soft childish voice pleaded.

"I'm not going to leave you," Nancy reassured her.

"Thank you."

"Good night, Rita, sweet dreams."

Nancy lay on the chaise lounge and pulled a blanket over herself. For Rita, whiskey and pills were a bad combination, especially in her condition. Too bad Rita hadn't inherited Nancy's gene for alcohol aversion.

When Nancy went out, a tonic water and lime were easy enough to handle, and looked like an alcoholic drink. If only Rita could learn not to mix her medicine with alcohol, she'd be fine, most of the time.

A pale moon filtered through the curtains. Nancy lay there listening to her sister toss and turn. She couldn't sleep either, thinking about all that had happened that evening.

"Are you in love with Sam?" Rita called from across the room.

"Yes," Nancy replied.

"I thought you were. I'm not in love with him. He's nice to have around and treats me like a lady," Rita said.

"Then you wouldn't mind if I went out with him if he asked me?" Nancy kept her fingers crossed under the blanket. How long would Rita stay in this friendly mood?

"Tonight I scared him off, and we parted ways. He likes you, and I'm sure he'll ask you out."

"Are you sure of what you're saying?" Nancy knew her sister's promises were like a fly in the wind, here one moment and gone the next, completely forgotten.

"Positive. I asked him if he was willing to leave the Navy, and he said no. I couldn't take his going out to sea and the long separations. It was bad enough with Dad gone all the time."

"Dad wasn't gone that much when he reached the higher ranks. He stayed close by us, even when Mom got ill." Nancy said.

"He was gone enough. I don't know how she stood it."

"She loved him and adjusted to it. That's what good Navy wives do."

"I need a man who is going to be around all the time. One I can lean on."

Rita definitely needed someone to lean on. Sam wouldn't be good for her. She needed someone like Joe who was home all the time and would be willing to take care of her. Too bad, she didn't consider Joe good enough.

Chapter Five

When Nancy was home, she liked to sleep late on the weekends. It was a luxury she didn't enjoy often when at school. It was late when she woke, and Rita was gone. Rita probably woke early and gone downstairs, not wanting to disturb her. The thought was good, but she doubted it.

She went downstairs to a quiet house. Mattie, their housekeeper, was just finishing up in the kitchen when she entered.

"Good morning, sleepy head."

"Good morning, Mattie. Where is everyone?" Nancy stifled a yawn.

"Jerry, Miss Sarah, their friend, and your sister went to Williamsburg for the day. Your Daddy is already hiding away in his office."

"Rita was up early?" Nancy was surprised.

She was as cheerful as a chirping bird," Mattie told her.

"That so?" Nancy sighed with relief.

It generally took Rita a few days to recover from her tantrums. Was it a good sign she was up and about or was Sam the reason? Was Rita telling her the truth when she said she wasn't interested in him? Nancy doubted it. It would be like Rita to let her get her hopes up, thinking she had a chance. It wasn't the first time Rita had lied to her. Of course, to Rita it wasn't lying. She'd just deny saying it. She had no intention of giving up Sam. Her sister said a lot of things and often denied saying them.

"She had another one of her spells?" Mattie said.

"You always seem to know, when she does."

"I've been around this family too long, not to know what's going on.

It isn't like Miss Rita to be bright and cheerful so early in the morning. It's this new man Mister Jerry brought home. It won't last long."

Mattie had been with the family for years and knew all the secrets. All the while Mattie talked, she was fixing Nancy's breakfast. Nancy sat down and ate heartily of the pecan waffles, syrup, and bacon. For a few minutes, she forgot about her sister.

Finished eating, she sighed. "Last night was a dozy. My room is a mess, but I'll straighten it up."

"I'll do it like I always do. You go on and do whatever you planned to do today."

Nancy finished her coffee, got up, and hugged the older woman. "I don't know what we'd do without you, Mattie."

"You don't have to worry about it. I intend to be around a long time. I haven't given up on your sister yet, have I?"

"Thank goodness. We'd be lost without you."

Nancy left the kitchen and went to see her father in his office. The door was open, which meant she could enter, but she knocked to announce her presence.

"Dad," she called to him with a big smile on her face as she entered.

Her father looked up from his work and returned her smile. "Come in darling, you look awfully tired. Did you stay out too late last night?"

"Yes and no. I need to talk to you."

"I see it's something important. I think it's a good idea if you close the door. I doubt you want anyone to hear what you have to say."

"They've all gone off for the day and probably won't be home till later this evening."

"Including, Rita?"

"Yes. How do you know what I want to talk about?"

"Rita told us you were tired and wanted to sleep so she went off without you. I gather it was another one of her fabrications?"

"It was a good excuse for not wanting me tagging along."

"I presume something happened after you got home?"

"Rita raised havoc with my room again. You and Ruth weren't there to see how close Sam was holding me while we danced the tango. She was jealous as hell when he asked me to dance. Her outburst spoiled the evening for all of us."

"Ruth and I went to a movie and stopped at her place for coffee. The house was quiet when I returned."

"The tango has seductive and sultry moves," she reminded her father.

"Most tangos are meant to be that way. It's a beautiful dance. Your mother loved to tango." For a fleeting second, Nancy glimpsed sadness in her father's eyes.

"So do I, and Sam was great." A feeling of warmth at the thought of being in his arms overwhelmed her.

"So your sister made it clear she didn't like the way you and Sam melted together."

"After Sam and I came off the dance floor, you should have heard the remarks she made about me wanting to get under Sam's skin."

"She spoiled the evening for all of you and as usual didn't care as long as it hurt you," Edward said stroking his chin.

"On the way home, Tom said Rita was jealous of me. I know she is, and she has no reason to be."

"She is and always has been. I've no idea why. She's had more than her share of things. Your mother and I never played favorites. Rita received what you and your brother did."

"When I got home, I took a shower to ease the tension. Then, when I walked into my bedroom, she was tearing it apart. I let her vent her fury. Once it was over, she collapsed and apologized. I took her in my arms and rocked her to sleep like I always do and stayed with her. It was about four this morning when I finally slept."

"That's why you look so tired. When she has one of these seizures, it takes the starch out of all of us. I'll talk with Doctor Warner. He seems to do better with her than the others have, and I'll ask about changing her medicine. She refuses to follow orders, and it makes it hard on all of us. It's time she had another checkup, whether she wants one or not. I was hoping she was getting better, but I wonder if she ever will."

"Me too. I'm sure, she'll never change."

"I been thinking that too, but I'd hate to put her back in the hospital. I love you both very much. You know it's going to take time, especially when she digs in and stays stubborn. It wears us down." Her father sighed. "Enough about Rita. Now, what's the real reason you wanted to talk to me?"

"Sam."

"I thought so. You've been disappearing every time Jerry brings him home. Could the reason be you care for him?"

She got up, went behind the desk, and hugged her father. "I guess it's pretty obvious. I'm in love with him, and he doesn't even know I exist." She went back and sat down.

"I doubt it." Her father pushed his chair back and put his elbows on the chair arms and sat with his hands held in tent fashion. "You're like your mother when she met me."

"Rita and I discussed Sam last night. I asked her if she was serious about him, and she said no. I don't trust her. She's lied to me so many times."

Her father smiled at her. There's an old saying, your mother used a lot. If it's to be, it'll be. Give Sam time. Being around two beautiful women can confuse any man, even if one is flighty."

"He seems to be taken in by Rita's charm."

"For a while, he will be. I hate to say this about one of my daughters, but Rita is self-centered, selfish, and fickle. She believes the world revolves around her, and she thinks of no one but herself. Jason was smart to dump her. It's hard for someone to live with a person like your sister, as you already know. Sam's very conscious of your presence. He's at war with his feelings for you. The age difference may bother him. After what you told me about last night, I'm sure he's thinking the situation over. Especially, if Rita continues to act like she does."

"Am I that obvious in my feelings for Sam?" Nancy felt embarrassed.

"They are to someone who loves you," her father replied.

"Was it that way with you and Mom?"

"Yes, it was the same." Her father smiled, remembering. "There were times we'd talk a blue streak, and there were other times when words weren't necessary. It was that way all through our married life. The age difference never mattered. We communicated in our own way and loved and respected each other.

"If you've come to ask my advice, I think Sam is a good man, but you'll have to be patient. From what your brother told me, he was hurt pretty bad when his fiancé jilted him and has played the field since then. He makes no promises to the ladies he meets."

"Would you approve, if he asked me out?"

Her dad smiled at her. "Yes, I would."

"He's twelve years older."

"I was fifteen years older than your mother. Age has nothing to do with falling in love. It sneaks up on you when you least expect it."

"Thanks, Dad." She went around the desk to hug and kiss him again.

* * * *

When Nancy left, Edward realized how much she was like her mother. He thought of Sharon and their age difference. Yet it was a once in a lifetime shot, and their marriage had lasted 'till her death a few years ago. From the way Nancy acted, he knew the feelings she had for Sam were something special. Sometimes first love was the only true love.

He was fortunate to find another love with Ruth. She filled his life now. Both were quite comfortable in their relationship. Nancy knew Sam was different from the other men she dated. He hoped Sam felt the same way. She would have to be patient and wait for him to make a move.

He suspected in her heart, she hoped she wouldn't have to wait long.

Chapter Six

Every weekend Sam spent at the house brought Nancy closer to understanding her need for him. It was more than a feeling of desire. Deeply in love, her body ached with the want of him. Her need for him crowded to the surface whenever they came close to one another. Many times Nancy felt the urge to reach out and touch him, but didn't.

The way he looked at her told her he wanted her.

Sometimes at meals, she caught herself reaching for the same thing and their hands met. The thrill of his touch made her heart flutter. At other times, when they were sitting on the porch swing, their thighs touched sending a melting sensation through her. She loved Sam and wanted to feel his touch forever.

Rita had now tossed Sam aside and was dating Joe again along with a couple of other guys. She played the field, enjoying all the attention she received. She was finally getting back into the swing of things and appeared to be on an even keel for now.

Sam had never asked Nancy for a date. She dated others off and on. A tinge of jealousy showed in Sam's dark eyes when her friends came to visit or take her out.

Every time Tom came to the house and Sam was there, they were friendly and polite to each other like two tigers vying for the last piece of meat. Sam kept his distance and never made a move to tell Nancy how he felt. Deep down in her heart, she knew how much he loved her by the look in his eyes and the way he acted around her.

After being out with a group of friends, Nancy came home in a pensive mood. It was late, and she wasn't expecting to see anyone still awake. She was surprised to find Sam sitting in the kitchen, reading a book. Damn him. He looked so handsome in jeans and a tight tee shirt. Her body grew loose and disjointed at the sight of him.

"Where's Jerry?" Nancy tried not to let her happiness show.

"Everyone's in bed except us," he answered.

"Oh, what's keeping you up, a good book?" All she saw was a book and an empty bottle of ginger ale sitting on the table.

"You," he said, impatience foremost. "We have to talk."

"Me?" Nancy tried to appear relaxed, but her insides were like Jell-O.

"I know it's late. Will you go for a walk with me?"

A walk this late at night could mean many things. Her heart pounded.

"Why?"

She stood staring at him. Was he finally going to admit what was happening between them? Or was he going to tell her what she dreaded all along. She was too young for him.

"You know why."

A frisson of heat shot through her when he took her hand and held it. Outside, a light river breeze made the leaves whisper in tune with the peep of frogs, crickets, and other night insects. They walked along the river path and stopped by the old willow tree, still holding hands. She was content just being with Sam. What anyone else thought didn't matter. She remembered her father saying love had a way of bringing two people together, whether they wanted it or not.

The moonlight filtered through the willow branches, showering patterns' of lace over them. She would be content if all he did was hold her hand. Even if he never spoke the words, Nancy knew he loved her.

Another cool breeze wafted in from the river, making her shiver. He pulled her closer, and his body trembled with her nearness.

Nancy felt the beat of his heart through his shirt, as she pressed her palms against his chest. His kiss was friendly at first and not that of a lover. She pulled away and saw the sad look on his face. He was holding back, groping for the right words. Words to tell her he wasn't coming back.

She said them before he could. "You're going to tell me goodbye."

"I have to."

"Why?" She couldn't hold back the tears. His sturdy hands moved to her face. He wiped away each tear with the pad of his thumb.

"I've fallen in love with you, my 'Elegant Swan', with all my heart and soul. I hope you understand when I tell you, I'm not the man for you. I'm much too old and will probably go off to war soon. I won't leave you behind pinning for me. I don't want you waiting in the hope I'll come back safe and sound. It's a promise I can't keep. War is more unpredictable than life itself."

Nancy felt the light touch of his fingers on her lips and she leaned her head against his shoulder. His hand smoothed her hair. She tried to stem her tears. Did he know how much she loved him? Stepping back, she moved away. Her arms came up around his neck, and they kissed as she moved in closer. Passionate and wanton, her body melted into his.

"God, do you know what being close to you does to me?" he whispered.

Feverishly she absorbed all the heat that flowed from his body to hers and felt his need as much as her own. She saw the sad expression on his face. It was one she wouldn't forget as he pushed her gently away.

"I've told Jerry I won't be coming home with him anymore."

"Because of me." She looked at him, tears forming again.

"Your sister and I parted that night at the club when I told her it was you, I wanted. She laughed hysterically, slapped my face, and ran into the house." He stopped short, not wanting to tell her about the rest of her sister's reaction.

"You're a vibrant, beautiful young woman. What you feel for me is just infatuation. It'll blow over when you meet someone your own age, and you'll forget about me. I'm just somebody different from the guys you're used to dating."

"There's more to it." She tried to smile and speak at the same time. Her voice cracked. "Sam Arlington, you're afraid of me."

"Damn right I am! You short-circuit my system, and all my emotions go haywire when I'm around you. I lay in bed at night thinking of how wonderful it would be having you beside me, supporting me in all the things I do. If I stick around, I can't account for my actions. I love you and I won't do anything to hurt you."

"Does my loving you make any difference?" She heard the pain in his voice, and now she let him hear hers.

"It won't work." He released her, turned, and walked up the path to the house.

She watched Sam depart. He had made up his mind and nothing she said or did would change it. Her heart was heavy with his parting words ringing in her ears. For a while, she leaned against the tree and folded her arms across her chest. Tears flooded her face. An arrow had found its mark and pierced her heart. What about the hurt and the pain of wanting someone who said they didn't want you? Was this what love was all about? Was this what Rita felt like when Jason walked out and left her?

Nancy considered herself stronger than her sister. Sam was the only man for her. More tears trickled down her cheeks, and she quickly wiped them away. When she returned to the house, there was a note on the kitchen table from Sam telling everyone he had to leave.

Chapter Seven

Sam, unwilling to return to the farm, shared an apartment in town with Jerry. It afforded them privacy the ship and farm didn't. Sam couldn't keep his mind off Nancy. He took on extra duties to use his free time. He made up his mind to stay away from her until Jerry's wedding. The ache in his heart for her was so intense it was driving him frantic and haunted his waking hours. His dreams overflowed with her dark sensual beauty.

He found a gold charm shaped like a swan in the Navy exchange and bought it for her. He would see her at the wedding and give it to her then, as a parting gift. It was something to remember him by. His thoughts were all mixed up. No matter what he tried, her sad face was always with him, reminding him of the words she hadn't wanted to hear and the lie he had told her.

He'd said he didn't want to see her because she was too young, and now he brought her a gift to remember him by. Boy, he was a goner. Sam's fellow officers didn't understand his changing moods and teased him. Miserable was too mild a word to describe him. One Friday night he at last accepted their invitation to meet them for dinner and visit some nightclubs at the beach, thinking it might cheer him up.

The Sand Dollar was located in one of the big oceanfront hotels on the boardwalk. This Friday night, the club featured the hottest band in town and was the 'in' place for young adults to be. The place was packed and the crowd jumping. It had been a long time since he had done something like this. Now, he felt old and out of place bar hopping. Most men his age were married or otherwise occupied. His friends didn't seem to mind having him along because there were plenty of women available.

The sound of music vibrated throughout the club. Sam's head pounded with the beat. The dim lights made seeing difficult. Couples chattered and necked in booths around the room. On the dance floor, hot, sweaty bodies moved in unison to the music's tempo.

The spring weather was still cool enough for Sam to wear snug fitting jeans and an old turtleneck sweater. Before he even made it to a table, a young woman approached him and rubbed wantonly against his body, sending an invitation he ignored.

She smiled up at him, hopeful. "How about it, handsome, wanna dance?"

"Thanks, but not right now." The blonde sulked and moved on.

After dinner, he sat at the bar with one of his friends and watched his other buddies operate.

The bartender approached them. "What will it be?"

"Make it a bourbon and ginger for my friend and a ginger ale and ice for me," Sam said.

The bartender raised an eyebrow, but didn't say a thing.

Sam's glance scanned the large room as he watched the dancers and the people around him with an attitude of indifference. Then, he saw her and his heart stopped. Short dark hair, a long neck, and a slim body swayed in tune with the music. He had memorized every line and curve of her body and longed to hold her.

She definitely was more than a one-night stand. She was the type of woman a man would keep forever, and he wanted her forever. He had stayed away, thinking his desire for her would wither, but it had only grown stronger. His muscles tightened, and his jaw set in a firm line.

"Hey, Sam what's the matter? You went tense all of a sudden," his buddy said.

"I think I just saw an old friend. I could be mistaken." He was going to find out for sure and turned to his friend. "I'll catch up with you later."

His friend grinned at him. "Go for it."

He left his seat at the bar and maneuvered around several couples on the dance floor. Why shouldn't Nancy come to a beach hangout? It was a popular place for young people. When she turned and saw him, a look of disbelief covered her face.

Sam maneuvered around a couple of admiring females and made his way to Nancy and her partner. He tapped her partner on the shoulder to cut in. The young man looked at Sam as though this stranger had no right to intrude on his territory.

"Shove off, buddy." The young man's attitude was condescending and meant to make Sam slink away, but his words only made Sam more determined to stand his ground.

"It's okay, Charlie. He's a friend," Nancy said.

"Kind of old for a friend, isn't he?" Charlie sounded upset that someone wanted to dance with his partner.

The young man's remark and look made Sam feel like he was as old as Methuselah. Nancy frowned at Charlie and stopped dancing and moved out of his arms. She smiled tentatively at Sam.

"Hello, Sam, long time, no see." Her voice sounded sweet and enticing. She came willingly into his arms.

Charlie stood by with a frown on his face, not wanting to leave. "If you don't want to dance with him, you don't have to. He's kind of old."

Nancy had known Charlie for a few months, and they had gotten along fine until now. She didn't like his attitude toward Sam. She knew Charlie was only three-years younger than Sam.

"Go way, Charlie, I want to dance with Sam." She hoped Charlie would accept her answer and leave.

She was eager to be with Sam. She smiled at him, and he returned her smile. It was one of promise. The band swung into a slow round when they finally started to dance. Sam pulled her close in a possessive way. Her body moved into his as if this was where it belonged. Being in Sam's arms was like being in haven.

This was the first time Nancy had bumped into him at the beach. "What are you doing here?" She tried to keep her voice calm and low.

"I'm trying to enjoy myself," he answered.

Nancy smiled up at him, knowing he was happy to see her. "It's one of the hottest bands in town. What are you doing here?" she repeated. She didn't wait for an answer and spoke again. "I didn't think you hung out at places like this."

"I don't, but I needed to get away. Sarcasm doesn't become you."

"How do you know what becomes me? You've never taken the time to find out."

"You don't know that, and let's not argue. It's getting late."

"It's early yet." She looked at her watch and up at him.

She fitted nicely into his arms and felt the warmth of his body against hers and relaxed. Tonight was turning out much better then she hoped.

He whispered in her ear, "I love you". She pulled away and looked up at him.

"You do?" A bewildered look appeared on her face. "Damn you, Sam, you're making my whole evening wonderful. I wasn't having a good time until you showed up."

"I'm glad," he said in a carefree way. "You looked surprised and happy to me." He smiled at her.

"Of course, I'm happy to see you," she replied.

"Are you?"

"Very much so, I was just about to call it an early night when you showed up."

"I'm glad I showed up when I did. Maybe we can take a walk along the boardwalk and talk."

They stopped dancing. He pulled her to the side of the dance floor.

"Talk about what?" Her heart skipped a beat. His hands were moist. She looked up at him, waiting.

"It's about you and me, my love." His words were decisive, and he took her hands in his.

"You're serious?"

"I've never been more serious as to how much I love you."

"You've missed me?" Her heart skipped several beats.

"More than you'll ever know. Let's get out of here."

"We can take that walk like you suggested." Nancy felt light hearted for the first time in weeks. "Let me tell my friends so they won't be wondering what happened to me."

While Nancy told her friends what was happening, Sam gave his buddies the high sign to go on without him.

On the boardwalk, they heard the surf as it crashed against the shore. The stars and moon shone bright as a silver dollar. The crisp night air hit once they were away from the club. Sam pulled her close to him as they walked.

"I stayed away because it's you I want and not your sister as I told you that night."

"I see." Nancy was happy to be with Sam and nothing else mattered.

"If you're worried, you needn't be. Rita and I parted friends. I just thought it would be better if I didn't visit for a while."

"What made you come to that decision?" She saw his face in shadow.

"There were several things. Rita watched everything you did, waiting for you to make the slightest mistake so she could lash out at you. Her jealousy would take over and she'd fly into a rage. I thought by my staying away, she would leave you alone."

"She does that when things aren't going her way. I'm used to her. She's my sister, and I'd rather talk about something else."

"Okay, let's talk about us."

"What about us?"

Sam stopped again and pulled her toward him. "I'd like to start dating you. Will your father object because of the difference in our ages? Your friend Charlie seems to think I'm too old for you."

She smiled up at him in the moonlight. "My father and I already discussed this. He was older than my mother, and they had a very happy life together. He doesn't mind. Don't I have a say in this matter since it concerns me?"

"You most definitely do."

"You can start dating me anytime. I think my father would be pleased."

He took her in his arms and kissed her, nibbling her lips and caressing her tongue. She returned his caresses and for moments, neither of them moved. Her hands explored, and he pushed her away.

"Damn it, woman do you know what you do to me?" He saw her smile. "When can I see you again?"

"I only go out on weekends because of school and homework." She had a feeling she might break the rule for Sam.

"I have to wait that long before I can see you again?"

"I have a couple of tests to study for, and you are a very powerful distraction. I'll be thinking about you more than I'll be studying."

"Good, as long as I know you're thinking about me, I can hold off until next weekend."

Time slipped by and it was later than she thought when they headed back to the bar to meet her friends. When they got there, the bartender told her friends had gone on to another club and she should meet them there.

"Damn, they've gone bar hopping, and I have no ride. My car is parked at Jodie's house downtown."

"If you don't mind, you can stay at our place tonight. I promise you'll have nothing to worry about. We can pick up your car in the morning."

"The apartment you and Jerry share?"

"Yes, I see you already know about it."

"How delicious. Jerry mentioned having a place at the beach and sharing it with you."

"You'll be perfectly safe." Sam saw Nancy's smile disappear. As much as he wanted her, he had no intention of taking her to bed, at least not yet.

Chapter Eight

In the apartment kitchen, Nancy and Sam sat staring at each other across the table not saying a word. Their heated looks could have started a bonfire while the coffee brewed.

Nancy broke the silence. "Do you hang out at the beach often?"

"No." His answer was emphatic.

"What do you do for excitement?" She was nervous, interested in everything about him, and wanted to know more.

"Spending my free time in night clubs with all the smoke and loud noise isn't my idea of fun, and I'm not a drinker. I prefer staying home and reading about the Civil War and history." I guess you can say I'm a bookworm or a homebody. When I return from sea duty, it's nice to have peace and quiet and no one demanding my time. I can do what I want without any interruptions."

"I see. Those are interesting subjects." She folded her hands in her lap.

"What about you?" He sipped his coffee.

"I like to dance as you already know. I go for the lighter stuff when I read. I like romances with happy endings, intrigue, mysteries." She felt her nervousness slipping away. It was easy talking to Sam.

"I like most flowers, except red roses they turn me off," Nancy continued. "I worked for a florist part time for a while, and after you de-thorn a thousand or two red roses for Valentine's Day, you get tired of seeing them. The pink ones or the white ones tinged with pink are lovely. I don't drink hard liquor or mixed drinks because they play havoc with my insides. Most people get headaches. I get a stomachache so I stick to tonic water and a slice of lime most of the time." She stopped talking, realizing she was chattering away.

"I missed you." Sam said.

She saw the hungry look in his eyes. "I missed you, too." It seemed right saying those words to him.

"I'm glad. Does the age difference matter to you?"

"I said earlier it doesn't matter to me. I've always been attracted to older men."

"I want to see more of you."

She sighed. "All you have to do is ask me."

Their eyes met in anticipation of their newfound intimacy. They talked about little things and drank coffee, prolonging their time together. Looks of longing passed between them, but both knew it was too soon.

Sam wanted her, but he also knew he'd do nothing about it tonight. He had waited this long, he could wait a while longer, even though his body kept telling him differently.

"I think we'd better go to bed because I'm on duty tomorrow and it's late." Did his words sound like an invitation? He hoped not.

"Good idea, which one is Jerry's room?"

"His room is the second door on the right. The bathroom is on your left and there are clean towels in the cupboard." Sam wanted to kiss her, but knew one kiss wouldn't be enough. It took all his will power to resist. "Good night, see you in the morning." He watched Nancy head to Jerry's room.

Sam paced the floor in his bedroom. His thoughts were on Nancy in the next room. He hadn't been able to keep his mind from her unhappy face the night he told her goodbye. He knew he loved her, but did he have the will power to keep his promise to himself and keep his hands off her? Sleep was as elusive as winning the main prize at the Navy and Marine Relief Fund drawing.

* * * *

Nancy heard Sam pacing before she finally fell asleep. Her dreams were haunted by the man in the next room, so close yet so far away. She knew when she accepted his offer to stay the night that nothing would happen. Not only because she was his friend's sister, but because he was that kind of man.

When she entered the kitchen the next morning, Sam was already dressed for work. He looked handsome in his khakis, and a longing ran down her spine when he approached and kissed her gently on the cheek. She had a half smile on her face, enjoying the feel of him as he put his arms around her.

"Coffee's nearly ready. I eat breakfast aboard ship. We have some Danish and bagels if you want them."

"Thank you, I'll be fine and get something when I get back to my apartment."

She wasn't sure how to proceed. God, he looked good enough to eat. She had to fall in love with a gentleman and one with principles. Her feelings were running in high gear. She wanted to drag him into the bedroom and make mad, passionate love to him. She knew she'd have to wait and be patient, but her heart demanded to know how long?

Sam released her. They stared at each other, and he smiled. It lit up his whole face.

"Good morning."

"Good morning" She returned his smile.

Tiredness etched his face. She knew he had little sleep. Dark smudges underlined his soft brown eyes.

"I heard you pacing. You couldn't sleep either."

"I had a lot on my mind."

Nancy felt the same and had hoped Sam would come to her during the night. She knew he wouldn't do anything against her wishes. Yet, she had desperately wanted him. Embarrassed at her thoughts, she looked away from him.

Neither was in a talkative mood and conversation lagged. The stillness created an awkward moment. Nancy wondered if this was what it was like after a couple made love for the first time, afraid to look at each other with a mixture of love, wanting, and regret. No, there would be no regrets with Sam.

"Coffee's ready." He shut off the pot, took two cups from the cupboard, and filled them.

Nancy went to the counter for the sugar and to the fridge for the milk. She put them on the table. Sam's hands circled her waist, pulling her to him, and she turned to face him.

He kissed her ear and then her neck. "It was hell last night knowing you were right next door."

"I know. I felt the same way." She leaned her head on his shoulder and waited. A flush burned her cheeks. They wanted each other.

"You know what I mean," he spoke in a husky voice.

"Yes, I wanted you, too."

"It's going to have to wait, my 'Elegant Swan'. Yes, that's a good name for you, you're my 'Elegant Swan'. I've never told you that you remind me of the elegant swans gracing the lakes in Europe."

He released her and walked away. He ran his hand through his hair and rubbed his neck.

"I want to make love to you, and I can't. I won't let myself take advantage of you." He stared out the kitchen window.

"I'm of age."

"I know, but you're so young." He leaned against the kitchen counter still rubbing his neck. "Desire isn't enough, and I'm damned if I'll take your virginity. I'm twelve years older and know better."

"I love you." She started toward him.

Then, they heard a noise outside and a key in the lock. They edged away from each other. Jerry came into the kitchen and stopped when he saw Nancy. Confusion appeared on his face.

"Well, hello, what are you doing here?" Looking more surprised than shocked, Jerry glanced from one to the other. "I'm not going to ask what's happening. The two of you look guilty as sin, and it presents interesting possibilities."

"Nothing happened," Sam said. "We bumped into each other at the beach last night, and she missed her ride."

"That sounds reasonable enough." Jerry still watched them. "You went to the beach?" He stared at Sam with surprise. "You never go there."

"Yeah, I knew you'd be spending the weekend with Sarah. So, I decided to go out with Tony and a few of the guys for dinner down on the strip and bumped into your sister." Why did he feel so uneasy, telling Jerry what happened last night?

"I missed my ride, and Sam was kind enough to bring me here. He offered me your bed because he knew you were with Sarah and wouldn't be here for the weekend. Nothing happened."

"By the look on your faces, maybe something should have happened. I've never seen a couple as miserable looking as you two are right now. I'm just remembering the old saying about handsome, lecherous Navy Officers and pretty young women." He laughed as he said it.

"Sam is always a perfect gentleman." Nancy answered sweetly, but with a sarcastic edge to her voice wishing something had happened.

"Oh really?" Jerry's grin got bigger. "I'm going to have to explain the facts of life to you, old buddy."

The mischievous look on Jerry's face told them he was enjoying their embarrassment. He finally stopped laughing and took pity on them.

"I guess Sam told you we share this apartment. I couldn't very well take Sarah home to the farm when we wanted to be alone."

Nancy's eyes widened with a smile of happiness and understood her brother's problem.

"Jerry, will you see Nancy gets to her car? I'm running late and have some work to finish aboard ship."

"Sure, there's no problem."

"I'll see you at the wedding," was all Sam said to her.

He picked up his hat and walked out of the apartment, leaving Nancy and Jerry alone. Again, Sam was gone from her life.

Her brother took her in his arms and held her. "I saw the look on your face. You've really falling for the guy."

She nodded and tears ran down her cheeks. She wiped them away with the back of her hand and tried to smile. "I love him, and he's the only man I want." Her voice cracked as she spoke.

"He loves you, too. Both of you looked miserable. Maybe, something should have happened."

Young in age, Nancy considered herself every bit a woman, though Rita didn't agree. So, when she returned home, she didn't tell Rita about her meeting with Sam. It was a secret she held close to her heart. Rita would only make fun of her for fantasizing about him. She wondered if Rita could ever love someone other than herself.

An Elegant Swan

There were times when Nancy couldn't believe she had a beautiful, self-indulgent, and unhappy sister. Luckily, Nancy could handle herself in any situation, but with Sam she would have to be careful and patient.

* * * *

The day of Jerry's wedding arrived at last. Sam had been polite and friendly at the rehearsal dinner last night. Jerry and her father were the only ones who knew they were dating. She hadn't told Rita for fear of the consequences. Anyway, she would blame Nancy for stealing Sam from her. He had joined in the conversations with Nancy and the other ushers and bridal attendants.

Saturday afternoon at the church, Nancy saw Sam for the first time in his dress whites and carrying his ceremonial sword. It made her heart seesaw and wished she had been the maid of honor and walked back down the aisle with him. Instead, she was a bridesmaid, who had to walk with someone else. A tinge of jealousy hit when she saw another woman holding his arm and looking up at him with stars in her eyes. She refused to let her feelings show, content with knowing he belonged to her. Being possessive wasn't like her. Patience was necessary and patient she would be, even if it killed her.

At the reception, she watched as Sam did his duty dances and ached inside while waiting for him to come to her. Meanwhile, she danced with the other ushers and old friends, one of whom was Tom.

"The blue gown flatters you," Tom said. "It makes you look more like a woman than a college kid."

His remark annoyed her. "I am a woman, even if you don't believe it. Thank you for the off-handed compliment, Tom."

"I see Sam isn't beating a path to be with you."

"My turn will come," she replied in a positive voice.

"Will it?" Tom looked doubtful. "It looks like he's deliberately avoiding you and being overly chummy with Rita."

"He can dance with anyone he wants."

She refused to let the thought of Sam holding Rita in his arms bother her. However, as much as she tried, it did. Rita had said she wasn't interested in Sam, but the way she acted told Nancy a different story. Why couldn't she be satisfied with Joe and keep her hands off Sam?

"I don't like to say it, but I told you so."

She pulled away from Tom and looked him straight in the eyes. "Stop gloating just because you think you're right about Sam," she said in a cool calculated voice, low enough so no one else could hear.

"Would I gloat?" he said, smugly.

"Yes, you would and enjoy every minute of it, thinking you had won." She frowned at him.

"I'm sorry, I didn't mean to sound that way."

"Didn't you? It still won't bring us any closer. You're like a brother, and that's the way it will always be."

"Doesn't this prove I'm right?"

"Don't be such an egotistical jackass." She broke away and left him standing in the middle of the dance floor. She should have felt sorry for him, but she didn't.

Nancy already knew Sam wanted her despite not having seen him for a couple of weeks. They talked continually on the telephone, and she could wait longer for him to hold her in his arms. Maybe after today their waiting would be over. Whenever she looked at him, she saw the thrill of anticipation in his eyes and realized he had made up his mind to make love to her.

Nancy knew Sam, like a jealous lover, covertly watched every man and fellow officer she danced with, and especially Tom. He had looked pleased when he saw her leave Tom in the middle of the dance floor. Could he be jealous? Maybe a little, but she doubted it. He was too self-assured and knew what he wanted out of life. Yet, when it came to her it was different.

She knew Tom watched her too, and she would like to wipe that knowing look off his face. However, she knew she wouldn't. They often disagreed and argued about politics and other things, but he was still a family friend.

Dancing with her father, she spoke of her concerns. "Will he ever get finished with his obligated dances?" Despite her impatience, she smiled at her father.

"Give Sam time, he had a lot of courtesy dances to perform. Most men like to save the best till last."

"Did you and Mom go through times like this?"

"All lovers do. There are times when you're so sure about your love for each other, and then there are times when you wonder if you're doing the right thing. It all works out in the end."

"Last night was the first time I've seen him in two weeks."

"Oh?"

"We bumped into each other at the beach a few weeks ago and have been talking on the phone every night."

"I see." Her father smiled.

"I love him."

"I know you do, darling. I think Sam loves you too. Only don't rush things."

"I honestly tried not to fall in love with him."

"I know you did, but sometimes these things just happen. The way you two are trying to pretend not to notice each other is noticeable to those who love you. I'd say you're both fighting a losing battle. Your mother and I found true happiness, and, if you think Sam's the one, go for him."

Nancy was so engrossed in conversation with her father, she didn't see Sam approach.

"Excuse me, sir, do you mind if I claim your daughter for the rest of this dance?"

"I don't think I dare refuse." With a knowing smile, her father turned to her. "You don't mind do you?"

"Why should I mind? I'm trading one handsome man for another."

Both men looked at her and responded in unison, "Good."

Nancy smiled at Sam, and the smile he returned lit up his whole face. He took her in his arms and for a while held her at a safe distance, just looking at her before drawing her close.

"It's not working out."

"What isn't working out?" Nancy said, all innocence with a hint of mischief in her eyes.

Sam whispered close to her ear. "You know damn well what I mean and don't ever ask me to stay away from you again. I went crazy thinking about you."

"Did you?" she said, pleased with his answer.

With that last remark, Sam pulled her closer. "Whether anyone likes it or not, you belong to me."

Awestruck, again at Sam's sudden possessiveness, Nancy pulled back from his arms. "I don't belong to anyone."

"As of now you belong to me, and don't forget it."

She realized it worked both ways, and a glow of happiness ran though her veins. He belonged to her.

"Sam, you're crazy."

"I'm crazy in love with you and driving myself nuts trying to stay away from you, but it hasn't done any good. Just being near you turns my world upside down. Seeing you dancing with those other guys made me realize just how much I love and need you. I thought I'd better tell you before Tom tries to convince you I'm unworthy of you."

"Nothing Tom does or says would convince me you weren't the right man for me." She spoke with a sweet smile.

"Oh, but he would try."

"He already has, and it hasn't worked. I wonder why?"

"It's because of our love for each other."

Nancy was happy at Sam's admission. "I'd like to hear you say it again."

"I love you with all my heart, now and forever."

"Oh, Sam, I love you too."

"Can we leave this mad house and go someplace where we can be alone? So I can show you how much I love you."

Chapter Nine

That night after the wedding, they were alone in Sam's living room. Nancy stood close to him, and he couldn't keep his eyes off her. He hoped she would agree to his idea when he told her about it.

"Since Jerry and Sarah have found a place of their own, I'm going to keep the apartment," he said in a solemn voice.

"You are?" She looked pleased and surprised." It's a lovely place and in a good neighborhood." She moved around the room.

"I'm looking for a new roommate and don't plan on spending my time here alone."

"Oh? You have someone in mind?"

"You. I want to share it with you. Will you, my love?"

Her face changed from surprise to happiness. He pulled her closer and nuzzled her ear, sending shivers through her.

"Sam, I'd love to." There was no hesitation in her reply. She wrapped her arms around his neck and brought his mouth to hers.

He took her arms from around his neck. He reached into his pants pocket and brought out a small box and handed it to her.

"What's this?"

"I saw it in the exchange, and I couldn't resist buying it. It reminded me of you."

She opened the box and found a swan pendant on a gold chain. "Oh Sam, it's beautiful." She hugged him.

"Here, let me help you put it on." He turned her around, and took the pendant and snapped it around her neck. "Now you are truly my 'Elegant Swan'."

Sam kissed her, first on her lips and then her neck. "There is no one I'd rather share my life with than you," he whispered in a low husky voice. His body responded quickly to her heat, and he felt her softness.

"I love you and want to marry you." The words came from his heart as well as his soul. He wanted this woman forever.

Delighted with his proposal, Nancy felt his heart beat faster and gently pulled away. His love for her shone in his eyes.

"I love you too, and I will marry you."

Sam picked her up and carried her into his bedroom. He set her down on her feet and took her in his arms again.

"You don't know what it's been like, wanting you the last few months."

"It's been hard on me, too. I didn't get much studying done thinking about you. I did pass all my exams though," she whispered.

"I'm glad. I wouldn't want to be blamed for your failing them," he said seriously. His mouth traveled down her neck, cascading kisses along the way.

"No chance of that." She smiled up at him.

His mouth softly touched the top of her breasts, trailing light feathery kisses along the way and back up again to her lush lips. His hands slid across her shoulders, causing a surge of heat to run through her already hot body and setting her insides on fire. Then he reached down and unzipped the back of her gown as he eased it off her shoulders. He let it slip slowly to the floor all the while kissing and exploring her body. He sensed Nancy's nervousness and wondered if he was her first lover. Or had she had lovers before? He hoped she hadn't. He loved her so much it didn't matter.

Nancy reached over. Her hands shook as she undid the gold buttons on his white tunic and slipped it off his shoulders. Taking the time to fold it, she laid it across an armchair. Seductively, she ran her hands across and down his undershirt and lifted it up over his head. Her fingers roamed across the solid muscles of his chest and caressed their strength.

Sam undid the zipper on her bra slip and lifted it over her head and moved away. His eyes sparkled with the pleasure of knowing the lovely creature before him, standing half-naked in her lacy underpants would soon be his.

"Are you pleased with what you see?" Nervous, she folded her arms across her breasts.

"Yes." His eyes feasted on her loveliness, and he smiled. "Come here."

She went into his arms willingly as though it was the most natural thing to do.

* * * *

Nancy moved in with Sam and slowly adjusted to their new living arrangements. She remained an independent person, and Sam lost more than one argument. Yet, she always had his meal ready and never complained if he lay on the couch or put his feet up on the coffee table. He learned how to cook and take care of his uniforms. Before, he had always had them taken care of aboard ship. It was a whole new world with Nan.

They spent five beautiful months together. She continued with school, and Sam took some part-time courses that would help his career in the future. They spent all their free time together, making love and planning for the future. Those were the good times, and they made the most of them, knowing the war would eventually intrude into their lives.

Sam's birthday neared and Nancy pondered the question of what to buy him. One day while she was browsing in the exchange, a gold bracelet with the Navy Officer's Insignia on it caught her eye, and she brought it for Sam. There wasn't much room on the back so she kept the engraving simple. 'To Sam, 'Love Always, Nancy'.

Sam told her he didn't want to go out and celebrate his birthday. Nancy made his favorite meal of meatloaf, cheese sauce, baked potatoes, peas and carrots, and apple pie with ice cream for dessert. After dinner they put the leftovers away and loaded the dishwasher. Then they went into the living room to relax. She left Sam relaxing and went into the bedroom.

"Where are you going?" he called.

"I'll be back in a minute." She couldn't keep from smiling, but was a little worried he wouldn't like her gift.

When she returned, she was all smiles. "This is for you, my love." She handed him a ribbon-tied jewelers' box.

"What's this?" It pleased him, knowing she had gone to the trouble of buying him a gift.

"Your birthday present," Nancy bent down and kissed him.

Sam looked as happy as a puppy with a new toy. He turned the box around and shook it like a little kid.

"It won't bite, open it."

"You're sure?" He smiled.

"Stop teasing, just open it."

Very carefully he slipped the ribbon off the box and ripped off the paper. She saw his look of delight when he opened the box.

"It's handsome. I've always wanted one, but never found one I actually liked." He turned it over and read the inscription aloud. 'To Sam, Love Always, Nancy.' He reached over and grabbed her, pulling her close and smothering her with kisses.

"I love you with all my heart and soul." He was so emotional he could barely say the words.

"Oh, Sam, I know you do. Are you sure you like it?"

She was breathless as she tried to fasten it around his wrist. She tried to clasp it three or four times and the clasp wouldn't hold. Disappointed, she frowned.

"I'll take it back." She took it off the floor where it had fallen and put it back in the box on the coffee table.

The next day Nancy took it back to the jewelers. "It's a special clasp, and we don't carry it in stock. We'll have to send it back to the factory and that will take six to eight weeks," he informed her.

"Can you put a rush on it?"

"I'll do the best I can, but I can't guarantee it."

Nancy got the bracelet back five weeks later and Sam wore it for a while, but the clasp still wouldn't hold. He handed it back to her one night.

"You'd better take it back to the jeweler's. I almost lost it this afternoon, and it's something I don't want to lose."

Later that month her brother, Jerry, received orders to a carrier on the West Coast and ten days later Sam received orders to a ship heading to Vietnam. Sam never got to wear his bracelet again.

* * * *

An Elegant Swan

Sam and Nancy sold the apartment before he left, and she went home to live. Three months after Sam left, she learned she was pregnant. It was the happiest time of her life. She wrote Sam telling him the happy news only to be disappointed in not hearing from him. The days and weeks dragged on into months with no mail from him.

With the help of her father and Ruth, his lady friend, she managed to weather the first months of morning sickness. They buoyed her spirits. Her father was happy at the idea of having a grandbaby around the house.

When she did speak to Rita, it was a struggle. Every chance she got she accused Nancy of dirtying the family name and being a slut. She never considered what she had done to the family name.

One of the saddest times of her life occurred when the Navy informed the family of Jerry's death in a plane crash at sea. At the Memorial Service, the family mourned and a few words of condolence from Sam would have helped, but none came.

A lot happened the rest of that year. Nancy graduated from college. The arrival of her son, David pushed away some of the sadness, and brought much joy and happiness to her and her family.

Rita married Joe in a private ceremony, and they settled in the cottage at the end of the lane until their new house was built.

Tom was elected to the state senate. His offers of marriage ended when he learned Nancy was pregnant with Sam's baby. An up-and-coming senator needed a wife he could present in public without a blemished past. Thank goodness, she didn't fit that category anymore and life went on.

David was a good baby and caused no major problems for Nancy. Ruth offered to look him David if Nancy wanted to work.

A year after Nancy had been working at Owens Real Estate as a secretary, she started dating her boss, Roger Owens. He was one of the town's leading citizens and twenty-years her senior. It was a marriage of convenience for them both. He wanted someone to help him entertain and run his house. Roger loved her and David. To him, her affair with Sam was a thing of the past. He adopted David and treated him as his own.

Their time together was short and happy. Roger liked to play golf and one day had gone out with some friends. The police came and informed Nancy of his death from a heart attack brought on by stress and overwork. It seemed destined that the men in her life didn't stay long. After three years of marriage, Nancy was a widow.

Roger left his real estate business to Nancy and David for the happiness they had given him. Tom came around offering his condolences and his help to straighten out Roger's affairs. Nancy refused and hired a firm in Richmond to handle her affairs and to find a buyer for the business. They had several people who were interested and wanted to buy a well-established business. She sold the business to three of the agents who had been with the company a long time.

She invested the money in her and David's future. Now she could do any thing she wanted.

Unfortunately, the bridge between Nancy and Rita widened. She resented Nancy for having Sam's baby and David got all the attention Rita thought she deserved. When she came to the house, Nancy and her father never left her alone with David. Nancy devoted her time to her son and helping with the household chores.

Her father and Ruth married in a private ceremony with just a few close friends and family. The idea of her father giving someone else the attention Rita thought she deserved angered her, even though she was married to Joe.

Nancy's parents noticed her restlessness after Roger's death and the sale of the business.

"Darling you're wearing out the carpet," Edward said one day.

"Sorry, Dad. I'm so restless."

"Ruth and I noticed your unhappiness. What's the matter?"

"I want to be doing something. David is such a good child and no problem with all of us waiting on him. It's a wonder he isn't spoiled."

"You've always wanted to join the Navy. You can carry on the family tradition now that your brother is gone." Sadness showed in her father's eyes.

"I've always wanted to do it, but there are complications."

"I don't think you have to worry about that. Ruth and I will be happy to look after David."

* * * *

At first, her time in the Navy was like a nine to five-job. Ruth and her father still insisted on looking after David, and he thrived with their attention. Nancy was fortunate enough to get good duty stations and as David grew older, she had him with her some of the time. When it came for schooling, he told her he wanted to attend a military school. The ships and sea beckoned him. Like father, like son.

Her time at Tidewater NAS had been the best of all her stations. She was within two hours of home and saw her son when he had time off from school. Nancy knew eventually she would encounter Sam and the fireworks would start, but she couldn't predict when or prevent it.

Chapter Ten

Tidewater Naval Air Station, Virginia

The departments' new Commanding Officer had arrived. Captain Samuel David Arlington III, stern faced, and tired from the chopper's bumpy ride and his long flight from Tokyo, Japan.

The parade ground before him was a carpet of green velvet. Men and women stood at ease. The hot sun made their uniforms blend into a wavering mass of navy blue washed with gold and white. Pungent salt air from the nearby sea assailed his nostrils. The heat, too oppressive for early spring, made his blues cling to his body like a prickly second skin. The stiff collar of his starched white shirt rubbed against his neck. Whites or khakis would have been more appropriate in this unseasonable weather.

The lack of sleep also added to his unease. A feeling of apprehension nagged at him ever since he'd received orders to replace Captain Nelson who had taken ill. This was a temporary assignment because he had already submitted his papers for retirement. This was his first time back in the States in several years.

The Administrative Staff was the last to be inspected. They stood ready. The second Wave Officer was a striking blonde. Keep your mind on business, he scolded himself. The next Wave Officer standing to her right made him come to a sudden halt. He couldn't mistake that face because she still held a place in his heart and mind after all these years. That tall willowy brunette sent his feelings into a tailspin. Memories he had tried to forget for so long flooded back.

An Elegant Swan

* * * *

A fleeting glimpse of a skinny kid running to catch a fly ball flashed before him. Now, this officer's nametag read 'Nancy Smith-Owens'. He quickly corralled his straying thoughts and brought them back to the matter at hand.

Nancy's dark hair curled neatly below her hat. Hazel eyes in a paper-white face stared straight ahead, unseeing. Her slim body was rigid with control. Realizing he had paused too long in front of her, he spoke in a calm, controlled manner.

"How long have you been in the Navy, Lieutenant?"

She came to attention. "Ten years." She hesitated before adding, "sir."

Sweat soaked her uniform. A trickle ran down her neck.

"At ease Lieutenant, where are you from?"

"I'm from Smithfield, Virginia, sir."

"Are you related to the late Commandeer Jeremiah Smith?"

"Yes, sir. He was my brother."

"I was sorry to hear about his death."

"Thank you, sir."

"He was a good pilot and officer."

All this time she stood at rest and stared straight ahead, not showing any emotion. She wasn't like the girl he had fallen in love with years ago. Why was her nearness still affecting him this way? Behind him, Commander Kevin 'Mac' MacLane, his new Executive Officer, and old friend, waited. Sam let Mac attribute his long stop in front of Lieutenant Smith-Owens to fatigue.

His affair with Nancy had ended unhappily years ago. He could imagine the feelings she might be having at the unexpected sight of him. He couldn't let old feelings get in the way. She was a junior officer in his command. They would have to abide by the rules and regulations they swore to uphold. He moved out of her range of vision and released his breath slowly to not draw attention to his uneasiness.

He wanted to turn around and look back. The shock of seeing Nancy again and in uniform had badly jolted him. Yet she had loved the Navy as much as her father and brother. He hoped the discipline that had played an important part in his life helped by not revealing his true feelings.

He thought his desire for her had died years ago when he had married Elena. Now dying embers flamed again. Lieutenant Smith-Owens wasn't the least bit happy to see him either. She had some explaining to do. He hoped to find out why she had ended their relationship so coldly.

Like all new commands, unforeseen problems arise. Lieutenant Smith-Owens was one monumental problem he wasn't sure how to handle. She could cause more complications than he needed. Her nametag indicated she was married. Things wouldn't be too bad then. It would make it easier. One thing for sure, he wouldn't be able to ignore her during business hours or at social affairs. At least she hadn't married Senator Tom Brewster as her sister had written and told him.

Now he knew why he'd been so apprehensive about coming back to Tidewater. Nancy presence could complicate things. This would be his last command before retiring. He would have to talk to Nancy and let her know the past was forgotten, either transfer her, or quash his feelings for her. It had been ten years and it still wouldn't be an easy thing to do. He hadn't forgotten her so what made him think he could do it now?

Chapter Eleven

The Officer's Club U.S. Naval Station, Tidewater NAS, Virginia

At the Officer's Club after the inspection that afternoon, a large and jovial crowd of well-wishers waited to greet the new Captain. Behind the buffet tables, Sam saw wide glass doors open onto a patio with tables and chairs scattered about. The sand dunes and the beach lay a short distance away, welcoming the sea.

His fellow officers expressed their well wishes in the receiving line. He turned to see Nancy standing nearby. Unexpectedly, her nearness swamped him, and he felt captured by her scent. She was engaged in conversation with Mac and the pretty blonde female officer.

Nancy's uniform emphasized her slim figure, and his body reacted to her like pancakes to syrup. Damn, he didn't need this. He was old enough to know better and not let the memories bring back the pain of her betrayal.

He had been a full Lieutenant Commander then, and they had lived together for five months before he went to Vietnam. She had sworn her undying love and would marry him when he came back. He never heard from her again.

She never answered his letters. She'd ended their affair without any explanation. What difference did it make now?

He married two years later and had a beautiful daughter, Elizabeth, or 'Beth' as she liked to be called. His wife died of pneumonia a year after Elizabeth was born. Elizabeth and his housekeeper, Mrs. Doyle, would arrive soon. His daughter filled his life, or so he had thought until now.

As for Barbara, his current lover, it was probably over before it started. Barbara had come home to Memphis and was working in the family's Interior Decorating business. She had come for this special weekend, but things had changed between them. Beth had told him she didn't like Barbara and didn't think their relationship would last long. His daughter was right.

In the receiving line, Nancy's voice was low and sultry. It surprised him. It was nothing like the impersonal voice she had used earlier in the day.

Nancy was standing in front of him, and he frowned. Her hand was stretched out ready to shake his. Again, his mind had wandered. He scolded himself.

He took her hand in his and felt a remembered softness. Holding it sent a familiar jolt of heat through him. Why was he still holding her hand and not releasing it? Most of the people near were busy talking and not paying much attention to them except for 'Mac' and Lieutenant Thurston, the blonde. Nancy pulled her hand loose.

"Congratulations on your new command." She said, with a smile that filled his heart. She saw his unfocused look. "Are you all right, sir?"

For him, her concern came much too late. What was he thinking? He could have sworn she looked amused at his confusion.

"I'm fine, Lieutenant. It's been a long and tiring week."

"I hope you'll enjoy your tour here, sir." Her words sounded sincere.

If she meant it. Her smile could melt the coldest heart, but he would never to let her near his again. "I'm sure, like all new commands, it'll be full of surprises."

"I'm sure it will." She smiled back at him.

Out of the corner of his eye he was aware Commander MacLane and Lieutenant Thurston had moved closer. They were missing none of the interplay between Nancy and him. What would Mac do if he knew his new boss and the young Lieutenant had been in love many years ago?

* * * *

An Elegant Swan

Sam's new quarters were well furnished and for now, he had the ten-room house to himself. It seemed a waste for one man, a housekeeper, and a young girl.

Yet he would need the extra space when he entertained. He fixed himself a nightcap of bourbon and ginger, something he seldom did, but he needed something to cool down his warring thoughts. He walked out to the screened-in porch and settled into a lounge chair to listen to the music of the sea. The sound of the surf lapped lazily against the nearby shore. The moon rode high in the sky, sending its silver shaft of light down to meet the land and sea behind the dunes. He liked nights like this. Beth would love knowing they had another house close to the beach.

Sam tried to relax, but found he was too wired thinking about Nancy. He was tired and out of sorts after the long weeks he had just finished. His encounter with Nancy today upset him more than he wanted to admit. Her pretty face remained firm in the forefront of his mind.

Years ago, Nancy had caught his eye and his passion with her smile and freshness. Yet it was her sister he dated for a short time until he realized Rita wasn't the type of woman he wanted. It was the memory of Nancy's smile and laughter that got him through those first months in Vietnam and then there was nothing.

He had to put aside the past and think about now. The important thing right was how he was going to handle the present situation. Whatever he decided wouldn't be easy for either of them.

Nancy never had to do a thing, only be near and he reacted to her. Why did she still affect him?

He took another sip of the one drink he allowed himself when his mind was in turmoil, which wasn't often. The liquor slid smoothly down his throat. He hoped it would relax him enough to keep his mind from thinking about Nancy, but somehow he knew it wouldn't. He would allow himself just this one time to remember what it felt like to have her in his arms.

How could his body still ache for her after all these years and what she had done? After today, there would be no past, just the future. Their relationship would be strictly business, yet deep down in his heart he feared he was lying to himself. The old feeling of wanting her returned full force. Why did she have to come back into his life now?"

Chapter Twelve

Nancy planned to meet her date, Mike O'Brian, and some friends at the "O" club. It was a lot easier than having him come all the way out to the beach to pick her up. Once a month on Saturday nights, they would meet friends at the Club for the Lobster Feast. Sometimes these affairs got boisterous and having her own transportation meant she could leave when she wanted to. She couldn't break her date with Mike at the last minute, unless it was for a good reason. Seeing Sam was not a good enough reason. Maybe getting out tonight would take her mind off him. Seeing Sam yesterday for the first time in years had rattled her more than she expected.

She was nervous as she entered the club. After yesterday, the blue silk halter dress Nancy wore helped give her the confidence she needed and showed off her long legs. The sound of dance music and happy laughter floated from the dining room. Some people were already lining up for the buffet. Others milled about chatting with friends. She looked for Mike, but failed to see him.

Smiling, she stood near the dinning room entrance, nodded to friends, and accepted the appreciative stares of some fellow male officers all the while looking for Mike. He came up behind her and put his arms around her waist, bending forward to kiss her lightly on the cheek.

"Looking for me, I hope?" he said.

Nancy laughed. "I wasn't expecting you to sneak up on me like that." Turning around in his arms, she smiled up at him.

His dark blond hair, blue eyes, and athletic figure caught the eye of many women, but Mike was oblivious to his good looks. Beyond his shoulder, she saw Sam looking her way. Her smile faded.

What the hell was he doing here? Most senior officers avoided the club and only came for special occasions. Sam stared in her direction. When Nancy looked directly at him, his smile disappeared to be replaced by one of cold steel, leaving her chilled.

A beautiful well-groomed blonde stood at his side. When the woman spoke to him, he hesitated before turning to her with a brilliant smile. Was it his wife or just a possessive girlfriend? She couldn't remember if the base gossip said he was married or not. A stab of jealousy tore at her heart. Damn, this shouldn't be happening. Sam's nearness had always affected her, but why was it doing it now after all this time? Until her discharge came through, she would have to watch her step.

She slipped out of Mike's arms. More questions ran through her mind. Taking Mike's hand, she turned and walked into the room.

"Where's our table?" she said over her shoulder, smiling.

"Willis and Henrietta have a table at the back of the room."

They maneuvered around other couples until they reached their friends. Nancy and Mike sat down and chatted for a while before heading for the dance floor.

"Knowing you as well as I do, I'd say your thoughts were elsewhere tonight," Mike said as they danced.

"I'm just tired."

"It's more than that. You've been off in another world for some time now."

"What makes you say that?" Nancy was a little perturbed that her uneasiness was showing.

"The last few weeks you've been jumpy as a pregnant cat, and what's this bit about resigning your commission all of a sudden."

"It isn't so sudden, I've been thinking about it for months."

"You never mentioned it to me or any of your other friends."

"The reasons are mine and nobody else's business. I just think it's time, and you shouldn't worry. I decided to devote more time to David. I'm still young, and I want to do other things. It seems to be taking forever for my papers to come through."

"Maybe your papers got lost in the chain of command. It wouldn't be the first time someone's papers have been misplaced on purpose or mislaid."

"Why would someone do that?" His words startled her.

"You're a damn good officer. Any command would hate to lose you. Your sudden desire to leave surprised everyone, including Mac."

Learning of Sam's arrival to take over command had led her to her snap decision, but she wasn't about to tell him.

"I don't think you'll be happy."

"Why won't I be? It won't be easy, but I'll have time to spend with my son, and there's Senator Brewster's offer to work for him. I'll be learning something new." She would never accept Tom's offer.

"You're planning to work for Senator Brewster? He isn't liked much, and I wouldn't trust him as far as I could throw him."

"He's not such a bad guy, no worse than the others. I've known him all my life so why shouldn't I work for him?"

"I won't be there," he replied in a solemn voice.

"You can always come see me. I'll be staying at the beach house until it's sold. I'm looking for a house near my parents. My time will be taken up finding it and making it ready for David and me." She smiled at him.

The music changed to a tango, and they had no time for further conversation. Nancy concentrated on the dance so there was no time to talk or think of Sam, yet she pretended she was dancing with him. Now, why would she do that?

With only two other couples on the floor with them, they all had plenty of room to dance. The other couples had moved to the sidelines to watch, leaving them room to maneuver. When it ended, they accepted the applause with grace and flair. Then, she spotted Sam. She went stiff from the look on his face.

"Hey, what's the matter? You look like you're scared stiff."

"No, it's nothing. I just got a chill." She turned her face up to his and smiled.

The tango had been the first dance she and Sam had ever danced, and she couldn't bear to see the stoic look on his face. That night at the country club, her sister Rita's outbreak of jealousy had ruined it for her. It was a night she never forgot and now, for the first time since then, she danced the tango with another man. She tried to avoid the chilling look in Sam's eyes. This was going to be another night stamped in her memory forever.

Damn, what else could go wrong? The orchestra swung into a slower number giving the dancers the time needed to catch their breath.

"I'd say your problem was more personal than you want anyone to know," Mike whispered in her ear. "It's as if you're trying to run away from something or someone. Whatever it is, it isn't going to go away. You're going to have to face it."

"My life's an open book and there's nothing I'm running from. It's just your imagination." If only that was true.

"Is it?" He swung her out and around on the dance floor. The heat, humidity, and her nerves sapped her energy. She felt the sweat on her brow, or was it just her reaction to the events of the last two days and the thought of Sam's presence. She watched as other heated bodies gyrated on the dance floor to the frantic beat of the music. Sam danced with the lovely blonde and appeared attentive, but not overly so.

She made up her mind she was going to enjoy herself, even with Sam watching. He was the one who broke off their affair and hadn't the decency to write and tell her. He hadn't answered any of her letters after he went to Vietnam and probably hadn't given her another thought. She scolded herself for letting old feelings rush back to haunt her. There was no place in her life for him now. She had managed to survive all these years without him and she could still manage many more.

If only Sam wasn't David's father. Her mind drifted, and with all the noise, she didn't hear what Mike was saying.

"Nancy?" Mike looked at her in a strange way.

"What?" She struggled to remember what they were talking about.

"You haven't heard a word I've said. What's wrong?"

"Why should there be anything be wrong? I'm having a great time." A small voice inside called her a liar.

"Are you? You're miles away." He knew her well enough to know she wasn't telling him the truth.

"You said that before, and yes, I have a lot on my mind right now, but I'm having a good time. Honest, I am, Mike."

The music stopped and they joined the others back at the table. The group's conversation covered everything from the latest computer games, flight and sea duty assignments, who was going with whom, and other scuttlebutt.

To Nancy's dismay, Lieutenant Kelly Thurston showed up with a good-looking fly-boy from Jacksonville. Blonde, voluptuous, and always on the prowl, the nickname 'Thursty' fit her well. She knew where to find all the good-looking men, eligible or otherwise. They worked in the same office, but Nancy outranked her by a half a gold stripe and that aggravated the ambitious woman.

Thursty had made it her personal challenge to steal any guy Nancy dated. So far she hadn't been able to lure Mike away. He was the only guy Nancy cared for. Neither she nor Mike wanted any serious ties. No man, since Sam, had caught her fancy. Although there was animosity between Nancy and Thursty, they tolerated each other.

Another thing that bothered Thursty was Nancy owned her own home and lived off base at the beach. Nancy liked living ashore because it gave her the freedom to keep her personal life separate from her military life, and she could avoid Thursty in her off duty time.

Nancy and Mike had been friends for a couple of years. Mike, an F-14 pilot, was stationed at the airbase. Attached to a carrier fighter squadron, he would be going to sea again in a couple of months. He didn't need a woman like Thursty who liked the chase and not the prize.

Everybody was drinking and having a good time, except Nancy who didn't drink. She just wasn't in the mood to have a good time. Knowing Sam was around made her nervous, but she wasn't going to let it affect her appetite.

Mike turned to Nancy, "Come on let's go eat before all the good stuff is gone."

"That's a great idea."

They excused themselves to join the line for the buffet. "I hope some of the lobster is left by the time we get there," Mike whispered.

"I'm starving," Nancy said. "I was so busy at home I forgot to eat lunch."

She filled her plate full. On their way back to the table, she was holding her plate in front of her with both hands when someone jostled her. Her plate of food went flying all over the man in front of her as he turned around. In slow motion, she watched the food cascade down the front of Sam's sport jacket.

"Oh no," she cried out in dismay.

Sam glared at her and then his expression changed into one of astonishment.

Finally she gained her senses. "I'm so ... sorry, sir." Her voice faltered. Without thinking, she reached out with her napkin to wipe off his sport coat.

Sam's smoldering, dark hooded eyes raked over her. He grabbed her wrist and held it in a vice like grip for a minute and then let it go. Nancy saw the threatening look on his face, but he quickly turned on the most charming smile for everyone to see.

"I'm ... sorry, sir," she mumbled in a low voice.

"It's quite all right. Accidents happen. It's Lieutenant Smith-Owens if I remember correctly?"

"Yes, sir, it is."

A half smile showed on his lips. Why did he have to smile at her like that? She could tell he was seething underneath. It unsettled her even more. A busboy appeared and cleaned up the mess.

"You're excused, Lieutenant."

Turning to leave, Nancy collided with Mike. He took her arm and led her past the curious crowd that had gathered to watch the interchange between the Captain and the Lieutenant. Once away from the throng of people, Mike stopped.

"What the hell was that all about? In all the time I've known you, I've never seen you so flustered."

"He's my new commanding officer, and I'm not exactly making a great impression."

"So what? As he said, accidents happen. Or is there some other reason why you've gotten so nervous this last month or so that you're not telling me about? He's a good-looking man, and I presume all the single females on the base are vying for his attention." He looked at her, but didn't say anything more.

"No snide remarks, my friend." His comment hit her the wrong way. "I'm not in the mood for them."

To Nancy's annoyance, she saw Thursty, standing close by and knew she observed the whole incident. When they sat down, Thursty joked to the others.

"Nancy and our new captain are getting along famously."

"Stop it," Nancy seethed, but kept her voice friendly. "It was an accident."

"I should have accidents with a handsome man like that." Thursty laughed, implying more than she said.

"If anything, I'm at the top of his shit-list after that little episode," Nancy responded.

She watched as Thursty turned on that knowing smile of hers as if to say 'there is more to it than meets the eye.' She would milk Nancy's embarrassment for all it was worth. The guy she was with didn't seem to mind it when she started flirting with Mike. Mike getting mixed up with Thursty wasn't a good idea. He knew she liked the thrill of the chase. Once she got her man, she would drop him like a hot poker.

Mike didn't need that right now. He was still feeling the aftermath of the crash that killed his friend and left behind a pretty wife and two children. Mike went to see them often, and Nancy thought he might have a thing for Trina, the wife.

Tonight, Nancy had planned to tell him she no longer wanted to go out with him, but she changed her mind. Now that Sam was in the picture it might look like she was expecting something from the Captain. Besides, she might need a friend in the next few weeks. She didn't hear Thursty's comment until Mike whispered in her ear.

"Hey, daydreamer, come and join the rest of us."

"What did I miss?" Startled, Nancy looked at the faces around her.

Thursty spoke up, with that familiar smug look on her face. "I was telling them about yesterday afternoon's inspection and how Captain Arlington stopped to talk to you."

"I wasn't the only one." Nancy's temper was slowly surfacing, but she kept her cool. She didn't want to say something wrong and give more fodder for the gossipmongers.

"He stayed an awful long time talking to you and the others were all guys. The smile he turned on you was just for you."

"Thursty, he was just being polite, and you're being obnoxious as usual. He was furious with me for spilling food all over his jacket."

She thought to herself, if anything else happened tonight that had anything remotely to do with Sam, she'd be more then the chief topic of conversation for the next few weeks. The gossip about yesterday's inspection was already circulating around the base. By Monday, tonight's episode would add more juicy material to the stories.

Naval Bases were like any other civilian community when it came to rumors. The smaller the base was, the bigger the stories. Mike had finished off another drink.

Nancy grabbed his hand. "Let's dance." She needed to get away from Thursty.

"Sure, Babe." He used the word to annoy her, knowing she hated it.

"You know I don't like to be called that," Nancy said with a saccharin smile was meant to put him in his place.

"No problem, my love." His words were insincere.

"I'm not your love," she hissed back, annoyed at him.

"You're very sexy and beautiful tonight." His voice slurred over the words, as he pulled her closer. She moved back, showing her irritation with him being drunk.

"Mike, if you're going to slobber all over me, I'm leaving."

"Don't do that, the night's just beginning. I guess I've had a little too much to drink with the heat and all. It's getting to me." He took a handkerchief out of his pocket and wiped his brow.

"It's taking its toll on all of us." Although the air conditioning was going full blast, she too felt hot and sweaty.

"What's going on? The last few weeks you've been touchier than a hornet's nest. Is there someone else you're seeing and not telling me about?

"I've told you, nothing is going on."

"Maybe there's something in what Thursty says."

Nancy looked at him, appalled at his words. "Oh, really? It looks like he already has a ball and chain. Look at the way the blonde is holding on to him. She's well stacked."

"She didn't like the way you and the Captain looked at each other. Are you going to make a play for the old man?"

"Don't be ridiculous. Have you forgotten there's something known as the Military Code of Justice that forbids relationships between Senior and Junior Officers?" Sam was married or about to be.

"At forty-one, a man his age isn't considered old these days." Her words spilled out before she could stop them.

Mike frowned at her. "How the hell do you know how old he is?"

She had to think fast on that one. "I must have read it in the papers somewhere." Her answer seemed to satisfy him.

She had been in a lousy mood for weeks. She seldom got mad, but when she did, she blew. She hoped Mike would drop the subject.

"Please take me back to the table."

"Okay, Babe."

He getting annoying and knew it. It wouldn't do any good to get mad at him.

He gave her his boyish grin. "Anything you want, my sweet."

Tired and miserable, Nancy wanted to go home. They pushed their way across the crowded dance floor, back to their friends. The music had grown louder and people had to shout to hear each other. Drums echoed in her head. A throbbing headache threatened.

"I think I'd better go home, Mike. I'm getting a splitting headache."

"Do you really have to go?" he said regretfully.

"I'm tired. The heat and the music are getting to me." She didn't want to tell him the real reason for her headache.

Nancy said goodnight to everyone and excused herself. She stopped in the ladies room before leaving. It was empty. She bathed her face in cool water and took a couple of aspirins from her clutch, swallowing them with a cup of water. Nothing else could possibly go wrong this evening.

The strain of worrying about Sam drained her. Leaving the ladies room, she found the hallway darker than usual. Several lights were out. She stumbled as the heel of one shoe collapsed on her. She struggled to regain her balance.

Strong hands reached out to her. She knew those familiar hands as they steadied her. She didn't have to look up to know they belonged to Sam.

"Are you doing a little too much partying, Lieutenant?" he said.

His words hurt. "For your information, my heel broke. I still don't drink, sir," she responded with all the fury she could muster without being impertinent.

The lights flickered on. Sam raised an eyebrow at her outburst and released her.

"Then you had better watch your step, Lieutenant," he said in a charming voice.

It made her wonder if she heard him right. Was he referring to her shoe or something else? "I intend to, sir." Again she emphasized the sir.

Sam studied her reaction as he picked up her shoe and handed it to her. "The heel needs fixing," he said in a reserved manner.

Like she didn't know. She thought he'd put on a good show yesterday and tonight. The handsome Captain was formal and correct. He still knew how to make her heart dance without even trying.

No one else was in the hall. She reached down and took her other shoe off and straightened up.

"Good night, and thank you for your help and advice, sir," she said, using her formal junior officer's voice in her most professional manner.

Holding her head high she marched past him out into the main hall of the club barefooted and oblivious to the stares of the other guests.

* * * *

Sam watched Nancy leave the club and sighed. He knew the next few months weren't going to be easy. He returned to his table and Barbara. They left the club a while later .He was no longer in the mood for partying and guessed it showed.

Barbara was quiet on the way to her hotel. "Sam, we need to talk. Let's have a drink in the lounge."

The lounge wasn't crowded, and they found a table in a quiet corner.

He had an idea, but thought he had better ask. "What did you want to talk about?"

"To begin with our relationship isn't going very well. For one thing, your daughter's a sweet kid, but she doesn't like me. Besides, I'm not the motherly type. I have a thriving career and business in San Diego that I like very much. Being married to you would mean I would have to give it up and follow you wherever you were assigned. I've worked too hard to get where I am. I'm not good Navy wife material. I travel for business, but only when I must. I've met someone else in the trade. We've been seeing a lot of each other, and it's getting serious."

"So, you're ending our friendship."

"Yes, it's best this way. We can still be friends. I also think you have some unfinished business that needs to be settled."

"What do you mean by that?"

"You had a hard time keeping your eyes off that young lady in blue tonight. Who is she Sam?"

"Was it that obvious?" he said, surprised. "I'm generally pretty good at keeping my thoughts and feelings undercover."

"I suspect it was more surprise than anything that gave you away. Who is she, Sam?"

"Someone I knew long ago."

"She must have hurt you pretty bad."

"Yes, she did, and that's all I'm going to say on the subject."

"You're going to have some difficult times ahead, if you don't rein in your feelings. Your present situation doesn't help."

"I can handle it."

"Where the heart is concerned, it doesn't always go the way we want." Barbara got up from her chair and kissed him on the cheek.

"Good night and good luck, darling. You're going to need it. Don't worry about taking me to the airport tomorrow. I'll catch a cab."

Chapter Thirteen

Later that night, at home, Nancy's taut nerves were ready to snap after her encounter with Sam. Her clumsiness brought unwanted attention to both of them. Sam could handle being the center of attention even though he disliked it. The cold look in his eyes upset her more than spilling her dinner on him. Everybody at the club witnessed the incident. Most were amused at the situation. Others, sober faced, were shocked at her social blunder even though it was an accident.

One spiteful person like Thursty could turn an innocent situation into an ugly one. Sam knew they were being watched. The woman with him had glared at Nancy, sending an unspoken message. It was loud and clear. 'He's mine.'

Sam still affected her in a way he no longer had the right to. The feel of his hands on her brought back lost, loving memories.

Once, she had been his 'Elegant Swan.' Now, she felt more like the ugly duckling. She had tried so hard to forget him and his nickname for her. Her emotions, like a witch's cauldron, bubbled over with a mixture of feelings. A hot shower did little to settle her down. Her nightgown and robe clung to her cold body. The biggest shock was seeing Sam at the club with a pretty woman.

"Admit it you were jealous," she said aloud. "You were with Mike. Sam's still a handsome man and had every right to be there with a gorgeous woman." Nancy tried to quell the frisson of jealousy that reared its ugly head. Still, some of her irritation with him remained.

The sparks flying between them definitely would not make for a good working relationship. She had made the right choice by resigning her commission. Being around Sam for the duration of her remaining time at work presented a challenge above and beyond the call of duty.

Nancy felt as if she were like little iron chips being pulled to him by his powerful magnetism. Was he feeling the same emotions? She remembered all too vividly the time they lived together, and the nights when they made love.

Now there was their David, a son Sam knew nothing about. She had written and told him the good news and had been so happy at the thought of having his baby. Jubilation slowly turned to heartbreak when she received no phone calls or answers to her letters.

Nancy would always be tied to Sam. She was going to have to find a way to tell him about David, and it wasn't going to be easy. It also meant she had to talk to David and tell him things she had avoided in the past.

Sam had come back to haunt her. Why did her heart melt at the sight of him? "Samuel David Arlington, I don't want to go through the hell of loving you again!" she shouted. The words echoed through the empty house.

At the time of their affair, she was a civilian. Now, there could be repercussions. She was a junior officer under his command. If someone found out, there could be trouble. It wouldn't be hard to avoid each other with the difference in their ranks. So far that hadn't happened. Twice in two days they had come face to face. Both times she wanted to ask him why he never answered her letters, but knew she wouldn't do it. It wasn't the right place or time.

If Thursty learned of their previous relationship, she would be more than willing to make it sound sleazy. Yet she seemed to have mellowed in the last few months and acted more friendly towards mankind. Maybe she had a lover she wasn't talking about. That would be unusual for Thursty because she liked to advertise her conquests.

Nancy could take the heat and so could Sam, but what would it do to their careers? The logical part of her mind warned her to keep a level head and think the situation over. She had already put in her papers to resign so all she had to do was to wait and be patient. Yet, her heart kept telling her otherwise. For the first time, she was frightened.

The look in Sam's eyes said he despised her, but she didn't know why. The darkness of night gave way to the gray light of dawn before she fell into bed. One thought tumbled around in her mind. What would Sam do when he found out he had a son?

Chapter Fourteen

Almost falling in Sam's arms last night was humiliating and wonderful. Nancy remembered the feeling of his hands around her waist causing a ripple of pleasure and a desire she didn't want to acknowledge. Those feelings had once before resulted in the birth of their son.

Nancy loved David, and he loved her. They were more than just mother and son, they were friends. He understood her need for being in the Navy. Now she wondered what he would say when she told him she was resigning her commission.

He was so much like Sam and enjoyed the military school he attended in the western part of the state. Nancy had never lied to David about his father. Yet she hadn't exactly told him the truth either. Now, she wished she had made up some fanciful story about his father.

She had believed her chances of meeting Sam while she was in the service were slim to none. It was a large world out there. She had made it until now.

The early morning sun was warm when Nancy went for a long swim in the bay. It helped soothe some of her inner turmoil, but she knew it to be the calm before the storm. Her attraction for Sam still lingered and placed her in a vulnerable position.

Back at the house, she tried to keep busy, but her mind kept returning to the events of last night. Later, the phone rang several times before she picked up the receiver. The low timbre of Sam's voice sent a sharp pain of unwanted heat through her. Damn, why couldn't she have been out when he called? She didn't want to talk to him, but it was too late now.

"Nancy, this is Sam." His voice sounded sure and authoritative.

"Yes, I know." She gripped the phone. Her heart pounded at the sound of his voice.

He went on before she could say anything. "We need to talk." The commanding tone of his voice annoyed her.

"Don't talk to me like that." Rebellion filled her. "I'm not on duty now, nor do I have the need to talk to you." Anger surged through her.

"Listen to me," His sharp voice commanded. "I'm not going to argue with you over the phone. Our situation will be difficult enough. Can't we meet some place and talk?" A long pause followed.

"Nancy, do you hear me?" He sighed in frustration. "You're not making this easy." Anger filled his voice.

"Are you trying to ruin both of our careers? I don't want to hear anything you have to say today, tomorrow, or next week." She slammed the phone down in a fit of righteous indignation. Her temper was becoming more volatile as the day dragged on.

"Sam Arlington, I don't need you back my life," she shouted into the empty room. "Loving you hurts too damn much."

Venting her anger should have made her feel better, but it didn't. She was too antsy to stay in the house after Sam's call. She walked along the windswept shore, kicking up sand as she went, venting her anger. A storm was moving in from the south and a sliver of sun shone through dark threatening clouds as they danced across the sky. She tried to dodge the greedy droplets of spray that showered her body from the crashing waves. As the surf receded, she let the wet sand squish between her bare toes.

The feel of the chilly seawater helped refresh her cluttered mind and body. All she could think of was Sam and the love they once shared. Tears for the past and what might have been streaked her face.

She had hated Sam for his desertion and not letting her know why he never answered her letters. One moment she was elated and the next she was deflated. She couldn't explain the feelings squirming around inside her. The sight and thought of him fueled them. A feeling with the name of desire entered her mind. That could lead to more trouble. Wanting to see him would be disastrous for both of them. It was an improbable, impossible situation.

After eight months and still no mail, she had accepted he wasn't coming back to her. Her moods had swung from happiness at the thought of her baby and then to complete desolation. It wasn't easy breaking the news to her parents that she was pregnant with Sam's baby.

Her father and Ruth were excited at the news of having a grandbaby in the house because her father had missed much of her and her siblings growing up. They now had the chance to spoil their grandchild.

Joe had left Rita even though he loved her. She wore him out, and the marriage hadn't lasted long. She lived in the cottage at the top of the lane and hated Nancy for being pregnant with Sam's baby. She had lied to her about not wanting Sam and claimed Nancy stole him away from her.

In her jealousy, Rita grew meaner and nastier toward Nancy and David. The family made sure she was never alone with the baby.

Chapter Fifteen

Having money and loving parents made Nancy more fortunate than other girls in the same situation. Still, a cloud of desolation overtook them all with the news of Jerry's death in a plane crash at sea. The family mourned his loss with a memorial service, but still no word came from Sam. Two months later, the arrival of her son, David, brought new life and joy to the family.

As for her sister, the bridge between them widened, and Nancy finally gave up trying.

Absent mindedly, her thoughts still in the past, Nancy bumped into an old piling, bringing her to an abrupt halt and back to the present. She let out a sigh and turned around for the long walk back. Lost in thought, her biggest concern was when and how she was going to tell Sam about David. The timing had to be right. She couldn't just blurt it out. When Sam found out about David, he'd fight her tooth and nail for him. She didn't want David to be hurt and torn between his parents. It was tough enough to grow up without a father, but David had managed well. How would he react to knowing Sam was his father?

Next week she would have to talk to Commander MacLane and find out what was delaying her discharge papers. Her survival in the next few weeks depended on the type of Commanding Officer Sam was. Did he sit at his desk all day, or was he a take-charge type of man, wanting to know everything that happened in his department? If he was the former, she had nothing to worry about. She would probably only see him at meetings or social affairs. Either way she would have to walk a tight rope and be careful in everything she did.

An Elegant Swan

A few months ago, her old friend, Senator Tom Brewster, had offered her a high-paying job if she would resign her commission and work for him. She wasn't interested in him or his politics. After all these years, she still felt nothing but friendship for Tom. There were times she didn't even feel that. Tom hadn't give up trying.

She wouldn't give up a career she loved for Tom, and yet she was willing to give it up for Sam, the two men in her life. One wanted her, the other didn't. She didn't know what to do about Sam. How would Tom react when he learned Sam was back? He wouldn't like it after losing out to Sam years ago.

It was growing cooler. The sun had hidden behind rain-soaked clouds, and she felt the beginning of the storm. She started to run, hoping to make it to the house before the rain came in earnest. With her head down against the wind, she ran and was out of breath and almost to the house when she stopped.

Chapter Sixteen

Looking up, she saw Sam standing on the patio of her house, with the wind blowing his dark hair. He was watching her and waiting. Why didn't he stay away like she asked? He stared, not saying a word. His tall imposing figure loomed against the gray light. Unwanted feelings for the man she had once loved swam to the surface. Dark colored sunglasses hid his eyes. How long had he been standing there watching and waiting?

Worn jeans accentuated his muscular legs and a turtleneck sweater stretched across his chest. His suntanned face reminded her of a rough-cut diamond. When he slipped off his glasses, she read mixed emotions in his smoldering eyes. He let out a wolfish growl, which was all too familiar, but made her uneasy. Sam didn't move and his gaze drank in every part of her, like a man adrift in a lifeboat for days without water.

"What did you expect to see? A sweet and innocent eighteen year old," she demanded in an unfriendly voice.

"I loved that innocent young woman."

She heard the sharp edge to his words.

"I thought you loved me, but it didn't take long for me to find out otherwise."

"What do you mean? I loved you," Nancy protested.

Memories floated, surfaced, and took her breath away. Her body tingled with the nearness of him. She tried to hold down the bubbling sensations in her body. She climbed the few steps to the deck.

Catching a breath, she forced herself to speak. "Did it occur to you I might have a date, or have other plans for today?"

"Lieutenant O'Brian has the duty, and he won't be off until eight hundred hours, tomorrow morning. I know nothing about your personal life."

"Damn it, Sam, why did you come? If anyone sees you, we both could be in a lot of trouble. Please leave."

"Not until I get some answers. You know damn well why I came. I need the answer to one question." His voice was low and calculating as he moved closer.

"Stop staring at me." She too wanted to know the answer to a few questions.

"You used to love it when I caressed your body with my eyes. I still appreciate a beautiful woman. So now I'm too old."

"I never considered you old." She was twenty-eight now, and he was forty. Her uneasiness at his presence eased. Maybe they would get things straightened out so they could get on with their lives. She still wanted to hit him for all the unhappiness he had caused her.

"Damn you, Sam Arlington." Cheeks flushed, Nancy glared at him.

"Temper, temper, you never used to have one, my love." Sam spoke in a calm voice.

"My temper is going to do a lot more than show, and I'm not your love," she threw back at him.

"You'll always be my love." The words were hardly audible.

Astounded by his soft-spoken words, she didn't know what to say, and headed for the sliding glass doors. "You might as well come inside. It's going to pour any minute now."

"Thank you." He appeared relieved to be invited inside.

The clouds opened with a deluge of rain. Closing the doors behind them, they paused to catch their breath.

Wary as a cat, Nancy faced Sam. Raindrops ran down her cheeks. She'd thought Friday afternoon's reaction to him was a fluke, but his nearness was doing it again. The tightness inside her curled with want. Damn, she didn't want his nearness to affect her this way. She had fought so hard to forget him and thought she'd won the battle. She should have known better.

Nancy wondered if the raindrops could have been tears of happiness. The pink buds of her breasts had hardened from the cold rain, and they strained against her wet cotton tee shirt.

She stood, entranced at the sight of Sam. His damp jeans stretched across his thighs clinging like plastic wrap to his muscled body. His tongue peeked out as he licked his lips with a slow sensual motion. A whiff of his pine-scented shaving lotion inflamed her senses. Her body ached for the feel of him.

Damn, she didn't need this. What was the matter with her? This wasn't supposed to be happening. She shook her head and broke the magnetic spell that held them.

"You can use the towels in the spare bathroom down the hall." Nancy turned quickly towards her bedroom and closed the door behind her. She dried herself with a fluffy towel, then blow dried her hair, and slipped into a blue slack outfit.

Sam was waiting for her in the den. "I see you still like the lived-in look."

"Still the same." Was it the beginning of a smile she saw on his face? "A house is to live in. I gather you're still neat as a pin, a place for everything and everything in its place."

"Afraid so. You know the Navy frowns on untidiness, especially aboard ship. There's no room for extras."

"Why did you come? I told you not to."

"No one will find out. I rented a car because mine hasn't arrived yet, and I called from outside the base."

In the den, she tried to ignore everything about him as she knelt down to put more wood on the fire she had banked before she left for her walk.

"Here, let me do that." He dropped beside her.

"I'm quite capable of doing it myself." She didn't want him near her.

"I know you're capable of many things."

She ignored the snide remark as his nearness sent her feelings and emotions reeling. It didn't seem to bother Sam that they were so close together, and he stayed alongside her as they rebuilt the fire. Their thighs touched again, sending a jolt of yearning through her. Her feelings shouldn't be double-crossing her after all the unhappiness he caused her.

She had waited a long time for this moment. She wanted answers and then she'd tell him to leave. She was already succumbing to his nearness.

"Would you like a drink?" When she started to rise, he helped her. His touch swamped her senses.

"Coffee, if you have it." He smiled at her.

"Instant? Do you still drink it black?"

His smile warmed her insides another degree or two. "Old habits die hard."

Was there more meaning to what he was saying? Nancy went into the kitchen and fixed two mugs of coffee in the microwave. She added sugar and cream to hers and brought them back to the den. Sam had settled into one of the lounge chairs and set his mug on the end table beside him. She sat on the couch opposite, waiting for him to speak. She fingered her cup and wondered if Sam was as nervous as she was.

After taking a few sips of coffee, he put his mug down. He got up from the lounge chair and crossed the room to the couch where she sat. He joined her and rested his arm carelessly over the back of the couch.

"Can we talk without upsetting each other?" He spoke in a friendly voice.

"You're the one who wanted to talk. What do you want to hear? That I'm still madly in love with you? Well, I'm not. I believed you when you said you'd come back to me and you didn't." She was upset and all the old hurts came tumbling out.

"Why weren't you man enough to write and tell me you no longer loved me. I wrote to you every other day and received no answer and no telephone calls in return. You didn't even send a sympathy card or note when Jerry was killed. You were his friend and best man at his wedding." She wasn't giving him a chance to get a word in edgewise.

"I loved you, but you knew that." She stopped her tirade and her voice lowered to a whisper. "I really loved you."

"I wanted you very much. I did love you. I proposed to you again in one of my letters. Weren't my letters enough?" He saw a scowl cross her face.

"I never received any letters from you." Her eyes never wavered from his.

"I presumed you weren't interested in marrying me when I received no answer to my second proposal. When I got ashore to a phone, the lines were long and the ear shattering static was so bad. Besides, I didn't have the time to wait to get a call through. After not hearing from you for several months, I finally gave up and quit writing. I had a feeling Tom had wormed his way back into your heart." Sam rose to pace the room.

"I don't believe you." She stood, fists clenched.

He stopped before her. "Believe me or not, I wrote." His retort was sharp and angry. "I sent you more letters than I'd written in my whole life. I told you how much I loved you and wanted to spend the rest of my life with you." He wiped his hand across his face.

"I never received a single letter from you." Nancy's eyes smarted from tears held back.

"Do you think I would stand here arguing with you if I hadn't written? I have no idea why you didn't receive my letters." His voice was loud.

"It's probably because you never wrote." Her anger now matched his.

"You wrote and I wrote, yet neither of us received the other's letters. I should have received at least one or two. Some should have gotten through."

"You know damn well I don't lie," Nancy said in a louder than usual voice.

"Then how come I received letters from Rita and none from you?"

"My sister?" Shock and disbelief filled her face.

"Yes, your sister."

"Rita never mentioned writing to you," Nancy said, surprised.

It sounded so strange. Rita picked up the mail most of the time. Had she deliberately stolen their letters? The idea had never occurred to her. Yet it might be the answer. Was Rita so jealous of the happiness she and Sam had shared?

"Rita?"

Sam's response to her words revealed the same thought had occurred to him. No. Even Rita wouldn't be so mean. It had to be someone else. She refused to consider Rita as the villain.

She tried for a friendlier tone. "We can't change the past. When you didn't come back, I finished college and went on with my life."

Sitting in a chair close to the windows, she listened to the incessant beat of the rain. Feelings so carefully buried surfaced faster than she was able to suppress them.

Sam came over and leaned down. He placed his hands on the arms of her chair. It took all her will power to stop from reaching up and pulling his face down to hers. The memory of the taste of his kisses left her warm and loved inside. He stood up and moved away. She got up and followed, stopping a few steps away from him.

"You married?" he said.

"Yes, I married, but our marriage only lasted three years. Roger died of a heart attack. We had a son David."

She felt like a traitor telling him this. Lying was something she didn't do. It weighed heavily in her chest, and the lump in her throat felt like a basketball.

"I was under the impression you married Tom."

"Tom is married to his politics and likes to play the field. My marriage was good while it lasted." Nancy wasn't going to tell him anymore than that for now. "Did you ever marry?"

"Yes, my wife died shortly after our daughter, Elizabeth, was born. The woman with me last night was a friend."

Why was he explaining to her about his friend? "She's beautiful." Nancy said.

"Yes, she is."

Couldn't he see the woman wanted to be more than a friend? She kept her thoughts to herself.

"Why did you join the Navy?" He was back to being the disciplined Navy officer.

It wasn't the question she expected him to ask. "I was restless after Roger and Jerry's deaths. I thought the Navy would make a good career. Unlike most jobs, I could put my teeth into this one. Computers are very challenging." She paused a moment.

"My father and my brother loved the Navy, so why shouldn't I? You can say I was carrying on a family tradition."

"I knew how close you were to Jerry. His untimely death must have upset you terribly."

"It was a shock to all of us, and we still miss him."

Nancy moved to the other side of the room and turned the music lower. She never liked coming home to an empty house so she always left it on when she walked. She swayed in rhythm to the soft music. It didn't bother her to know Sam watched her every move. Tiredness seeped through her body.

She turned to him. "Go away, Sam."

Instead, he came and took her in his arms, and they danced to the soft romantic music.

"We haven't solved our problem." His voice was low and lazy.

"You needn't worry. The past is over and done with, and it can't be changed. I won't say or do anything to hurt your career here."

"How can I be sure of that?" He appeared leery of accepting her quick answer.

"You'll just have to trust me." She tried to assure him again. Her mood was softening.

"Should I? The real reason why I came to see you was about the letters and the situation we face. It isn't going to be easy."

"No, it isn't."

"Seeing you at the inspection, so white and somber, didn't help either. I never expected to see you again."

"That makes two of us. You don't know how hard I tried to get out of that inspection. I couldn't think of a way to warn you."

He seemed to relax with her words. "Thank you for wanting to try. What happened between us in the past can't have any bearing on our present situation." His voice held that authoritative manner she knew so well.

"I understand. You needn't worry. As I said, I won't try to use our former relationship to my advantage. I've already put in my papers to resign my commission."

"We're going to have to be civil with each other whether we like it or not." His voice held enough sincerity to make her believe him.

His gaze wrapped her in a softness she didn't want to acknowledge. A face she once loved too much still haunted her every time she looked at their son. Now the memory was a reality, and all they could be to each other were friends and nothing more.

"You're cautious as always." She smiled, as if at a private joke.

They hadn't been cautious the night David had been conceived. Their passion had burned bright, and they'd been too much in love to realize that the precautions they took could go wrong. She never regretted it. What if he was telling the truth?

"Nancy, did you hear what I said?"

"Oh, yes. I presume you have plans to marry your friend, but my appearance has thrown a wrench in the works. The minute she wasn't around, you called me." Her voice was almost a hiss. "I feel sorry for her. Was she being bitchy?"

"Why should you feel sorry for her? We're just friends. She knows I have no intention of marrying her, and she's found someone else to love, an associate she works with." They stopped dancing.

"You know it's never going to be strictly business between us. What happened is still haunting you or you wouldn't be here." She wrapped her hands around her shoulders as shivers ran up and down her spine.

The possibility of him telling the truth found its way into her heart. Sam had no reason to lie, so why didn't she believe him?

"We've opened doors to the past we thought were closed for good," Nancy said. "I think after you arrived here and saw me, you realized things weren't going to be as black and white as you'd like them to be. My appearance threw a spinner into your orderly life, and you don't know how to handle it, but you will."

Nancy's attitude of being on the defensive was changing. She knew exactly how Sam felt, because she was feeling the same way. He would always be a part of her life, and she hoped she would always be part of his. Only time would tell.

Damn it. She thought she'd gotten him out of her system, and he could never touch her heart again. He reached for her and held her at arm's length.

"As long as you're in my command, it can't be any other way." His voice was gentle and decisive. With the feel of him, hot flames of desire, dormant for so long, flickered to life inside her. Would the flames smolder and die, or would Sam's nearness in the next few months fan them from glowing embers to raging flames? In this short time, her feelings had turned traitor. She wanted him as much as she had ever wanted him.

"I understand." She was solemn.

He let her go. "We'll work something out." His voice sounded tired.

"Will we, Captain?" Her emphasis on the word Captain brought back all the difficulties between them.

"I have to be Captain Arlington," he said in a calm, friendly tone. "You have to be Lieutenant Smith-Owens. Do you understand?"

"Yes, I understand more than you realize."

Why couldn't life be simple? She didn't need more complications. Sam within arms reach equated to a drug in her system she craved and had missed for so long. Now it was within reach and she couldn't have it. Damn the Navy and their regulations.

Chapter Seventeen

One minute, she wished Sam would leave now and the next she was pleased he came. It was another unanswered question to add to all the others roaming around in her fertile mind. The ringing phone startled her. She excused herself, and went to answer it.

The rain outside still fell in a steady downpour. The call was from David. She looked quickly towards Sam. He would hear her end of the conversation even though she kept her voice low.

"Yes, darling, I have company and everything's fine. I'll be able to spend next weekend with you."

"Mom, you sound funny. It's not Senator Brewster is it?"

"No, it isn't. It's an old friend who stopped by."

"You sure you're all right?"

Nancy darted furtive looks at Sam. All the while, he watched her, his brow stormy. She suspected he thought it was another lover. "Anything you plan will be fine with me. See you then, darling."

She put the receiver down and turned to Sam. His soft brown eyes had turned to splinters of steel. A smidgeon of dissatisfaction showed itself as his long fingers tightened around his coffee mug. Before she could resume their conversation and tell Sam, she was talking to her son, the telephone rang again. The look he gave her would freeze any junior officer in their tracks.

"Aren't you going to answer it?"

"Let it ring, it can't be important."

Her recorder clicked on. Tom's enthusiastic voice carried across the room. "Hi, love, I have some time before heading back north, thought I'd stop by in case you have nothing better to do. I'm on my way."

Nancy flinched at the sound of Tom's voice.

"Put on something special, I feel romantic tonight, Love you."

Damn Tom. Even though she hadn't answered the phone, he took it for granted she would be home because she generally was. He thought he had the right to stop by any time he liked and was obstinate as hell. Why did he keep calling her darling and love? He just wouldn't give up. Having Sam here caused her enough problems. She didn't need Tom to add more fuel to the fire. She could imagine what Sam's thought.

After last night with Mike, her son's recent call, and now Tom's, it sounded as though she had several lovers.

Sam bent over the coffee table and slammed down his mug. He stood and came very close, startling her.

"People talk about sailors having a girl in every port. What about you? How many men' are you home-porting?"

His remark stunned Nancy. Her hand came up to slap him, and he grabbed her wrist and held it. She was furious.

"If you're insinuating I'm sleeping around, you're sadly mistaken."

He released her wrist. Fury overtook her, and she slapped him hard across the jaw.

"Captain or no Captain, this is the second time in two days you've insulted me for no reason at all." She suckered punched him hard in the gut with her fist.

"Damn it, that hurt," He gripped his stomach, wincing from the unexpected blow.

Her hand vibrated from the force of her punch. It still didn't stop her from grabbing a fistful of his sweater and bringing his face level with hers.

"You conceited jackass." Her temper exploded. "What gives you the right to accuse me of sleeping around? There's only one sailor I ever home-ported, and it turned out to be the biggest mistake of my life."

She stopped in mid-sentence. It hadn't been the biggest mistake she ever made, but one of the most wonderful. She had her son David. She let go of his sweater. Sam hadn't picked up on her unfinished sentence.

"What I do and don't do in my private life is none of your business, and if you must know, the first call was from my son."

He looked surprised. She hoped that would satisfy him.

The front door chimes echoed through the house interrupting them. Damn Tom, that was all she needed. She went to answer the door, leaving Sam to nurse the spot where she hit him.

Tom followed Nancy into the den and didn't even take off his raincoat before trying to pull her into his arms and kiss her. She turned her cheek to avoid his kiss. Tom turned on his brightest smile when he saw Nancy had company and looked at her guest. His smile faded to a look of surprise.

His surprise at seeing Sam gave way to a calculating look. He took in everything about Sam before he spoke. "Well, Sam, this is a surprise. It's been a long time."

"You should know, Tom."

Tom turned to Nancy. "Why didn't you tell me Sam was here? I would have postponed my visit."

Who was Tom trying to kid? He knew she hadn't answered the phone.

"You didn't give me a chance."

Sam's imposing figure moved forward. Nancy smiled at Tom." Sam was just leaving."

Nancy saw the look on Tom's face, pretending to be dismayed at Sam's departure, but she knew better. They had acted like surly bantam roosters the first time they met.

"You're leaving, Sam," Nancy said firmly, hoping Sam would take the hint.

The look on both the men's faces told her they had dug in their heels and weren't about to give the other any room to maneuver.

"Are you renewing an old friendship?" Tom's words held a tinge of sarcasm.

"Nancy and I have unfinished business." Sam's bluntness caught her off guard.

Nancy started to say something, but Tom cut her off. "Yes, I can imagine you have a lot of old business to discuss. Do you like politics, Sam?"

"It depends on what kind you're talking about. The Navy has its own brand of politics."

"That's true. For an ambitious man like yourself, your association with a junior officer could hamper your future chances of making Rear Admiral."

"It's a possibility," Sam said. "However, there are only three people present, and I doubt either Nancy or I would jeopardize our careers over something that happened years ago before she joined the Navy. If word got out, there'd be only one person the finger would point to and that would be you, Tom. It wouldn't look too nice when your constituents found out you besmirched the family of one of your staunchest supporters. Or that you pulled a lot of strings to keep your competition overseas for as long as you could."

"You're saying Tom used his influence to keep us apart?" Nancy stared at her old friend.

Tom ignored the accusation as though it was of no importance.

"Why you SOB?" Nancy very seldom swore, but right now, she was steaming. "You were supposed to be my friend."

She had learned through the years he was only interested in himself, but she never thought he would stoop so low. He was only interested in people who could do things for him like her father.

Tom ignored her outburst. "Have you ever thought about retirement?"

"Have you?" came Sam's quick reply.

Nancy grew nervous guessing where Tom was headed. She needed to stop him before he went too far. She stepped between the two men.

"When you retire, look me up," Tom said to Sam. "I'm sure we can iron out our differences. I can always use a good man."

"It's nice of you to offer, Tom, but let's face it, you and I will never come to terms on any subject. I already have other plans for my retirement."

Sam watched as Tom reached for Nancy's hand and tried to take it in his own. She snatched it back and stepped away. Tom didn't like it.

"Tom, would you like some coffee? Sam?" She was desperate to calm both men down.

"That would be nice to take the chill off," Tom agreed.

"Sam?" She looked at him, but saw nothing in his face.

"No, thanks, I'm fine."

When Nancy returned from the kitchen and handed Tom his coffee, he reached for her hand again. She turned too quickly and bumped into Sam, knocking him off balance. He grabbed her shoulders and pulled her down with him onto the couch.

Tom looked on in astonishment at this turn of events. Nancy landed on top of Sam. Unwanted memories of other times together flooded back. She looked down and saw the familiar simmering passion in his eyes. His warm receptive arms wrapped around her and a familiar sound of pleasure escaped her. He was going to kiss her.

Panic stricken, she broke loose and rolled off of him and onto the floor. Nancy couldn't let herself want his kisses. She wouldn't let it happen again. Slightly dazed, she sat up and looked around. Oh, how she missed having his arms around her.

Tom watched their every move like a hawk and stored away the information for future use. He had powerful friends and the influence to hurt Sam's career, which he had already done by keeping Sam overseas this long. Tom hated to lose.

Tom's none too discreet cough broke her spell. She hadn't forgotten about Tom being there. After what had just happened, the satisfied look on his face annoyed her. She turned to look at Sam sitting on the couch while sexual desire still lingered in his eyes.

"Darling, you forgot to mention you and Sam are renewing your old relationship."

"We were doing no such thing," she snapped, then paused. "No. Dam it, I'm not going to do any explaining. You both can get the hell out of my house." She was furious with both of them.

"There's no need to swear, my dear," Tom said.

"Stop treating me, like a child. Damn you, Tom, it's your own fault if you didn't like what just happened. You shouldn't have come. It was an accident, and if you can't accept it as that, then you can leave." She wasn't going to let on she liked the feel of Sam's arms around her, knowing she shouldn't have. Her mind was a whirlpool of emotions after being so close to him.

"Sam, I hope you don't mind leaving? I have some important business I want to discuss with Nancy." Tom spoke in an authoritative voice.

Nancy glared at both men. She didn't like the way Tom was acting. The slight nod of her head told Sam it would be alright. Nancy knew Tom was watching her closely as she led Sam to the door and said good night.

"Are you going to be okay? Sam's voice showed his concern.

"I'll be fine," she assured him.

"We'll finish this conversation another time."

"That's fine with me. Good night."

Chapter Eighteen

Nancy saw Sam out the door and returned to the den, her emotions running in high gear. She went over and stood by the windows, not saying a word. She waited for Tom to stop pacing and speak.

"How interesting that Sam is back in town," Tom said, his voice full of innuendo.

"What do you mean?" Nancy wasn't in the mood to listen to him.

"After that blatant display on the couch, I would say you're still lovers."

"Don't be ridiculous. I haven't seen Sam in ten years, thanks to you." Nancy was determined she wouldn't let Tom know how she felt. "What are you implying, Tom? Are you trying to blackmail me? You think I still have feelings for the father of my son and who is now, my commanding officer. Blackmail is an ugly business. Don't even think of using it against me. You're used to getting what you want, but it won't work here. I know you too well."

"What are you talking about?" His face had gone pale, and he looked agitated. "Where did you get such a silly idea?"

"A long time ago, my mother taught me to keep a diary. It's a habit I still keep. You're not the only one who keeps track of their so-called friend's behavior. It would be interesting reading for your constituents if the tabloids got hold of my information. As long as you leave Sam and me alone, they will stay hidden under lock and key. If you try to cause any trouble, my papers will be sent to all the tabloids, and I'll show no mercy. You don't want me for an enemy."

"I see." He stared at her, clearly aware she meant every word she said.

"Sam also knows I have a son and believes it to be Roger's. When the time comes, I'll tell him the truth, but until then, don't get any ideas along that line. I can ruin your career just as easily as you can ruin mine. Since I'm getting out, you can't hurt me as much as I can hurt you."

"That wasn't very nice bumping into Sam the way you did."

"It was an accident." She managed to keep a straight face.

"You've had the boy all to yourself. It's going to be hard sharing him with a father you still love, but can't have."

"If I am still in love with Sam, it's none of your business. One kiss and a romp on the couch doesn't' spell love."

"You're in a difficult situation. Sam is your commanding officer. The woman he's dating has intentions of becoming Mrs. Samuel David Arlington the Third."

Nancy smirked. "So, you've had your spies at work again. However, your informants have got it wrong. She's in love with someone else, and they're just friends."

"I suppose Sam told you that."

"It doesn't matter where I got the information."

"I suppose you'd believe anything he told you."

"Why shouldn't I?"

"In my position, it's always good to know all the players in the game. I thought I had gotten rid of Sam by keeping him in billets overseas. I see I was mistaken."

"So that's what Sam meant when he said you should know." The words burst out of her. Nancy was mortified at what Tom now admitted. "You used your influence to keep him away from me. I bet you also had some help from my sister."

"Knowing the right people in my position helps. I do a colleague a favor, he does one in return. It can be very beneficial, especially when you know all their secrets, and they can't be traced back to you."

"We're back to the blackmailer. The name fits you like a glove." Despite acting as her friend, he was nothing but a self-centered SOB. She had known it for a long time, but hadn't wanted to accept it. "You deliberately used your influence to keep Sam overseas."

"It was easy keeping him overseas and away from you."

"How dare you? You had no right to interfere with my life. You never give up do you?"

Tom ignored her outburst. "No, I don't, and you're still in love with him whether you admit it or not."

She couldn't deny it. Anyway, Tom had seen them on the couch. Her heart tied itself in knots at the thought of Tom locking her out of Sam's life. Nancy stared at her once friend and would-be lover. His eyes were bright and knowing.

"You rat!"

"I lost you once to Sam, and I don't intend losing you again. I loved you and waited for you to grow up, hoping you'd forget him and realize I was the better man. I made it my business to know everything about Sam, including your affair with him. He's ambitious and in line for Rear Admiral. He won't let you interfere with that. If word gets out he's fooling around with a junior officer in his command, he can lose everything, and I don't think you'd like to see that happen. So, be careful, my dear."

"You're threatening me again?"

"As for this conversation, it's just between you and me. It's your word against mine, and I'm sure you know who will win. I have all the power and influence. I'm just letting you know where you stand."

"Like hell you are."

Her hand came up hard across his face. Her hands tighten into fists. "Did you tamper with our mail while Sam was in Vietnam?"

Tom rubbed his face. "I may stretch the truth and do some underhanded things, but I'm not foolish enough to tamper with the U.S. Mail."

"Then who did? We wrote each other, and neither of us received any mail from the other."

"You mentioned that before, and I just assumed it was the war."

"Some of our mail should have gotten through."

The look on Tom's face told her he knew something. "Why don't you ask your lovely sister? She had first crack at Sam and lost him to you. Didn't she collect the mail and take it to the box?" He had a know-it-all-look on his face.

"You're lying. My sister would never do anything as mean as that."

Nancy couldn't hide her frustration.

"Wouldn't she? The next time you're home, ask her."

"I don't believe you." She said, but it had occurred to her and Sam earlier.

"Your sister was always jealous of you, and what better way to get back at you, than steal your letters from the man she wanted and couldn't have?" Tom sounded sure of what he said.

"You're lying. She said she never wanted Sam." Nancy was tired and didn't want to believe Rita would stoop so low.

"Is that what she told you? You should know better. You're a bigger fool than I thought for believing her."

"Get out. I never want to see you again."

His last words were just too much for her to accept. Yet the more she considered it, the more she realized her sister could have done something like that and thought nothing of it.

Chapter Nineteen

Sam went back to an empty house with a feeling of disbelief and a thumping heart. What happened between him and Nancy was beginning to penetrate his muddled mind. Anything Tom thought wasn't important.

He wanted to kiss her and never let her go despite all that had happened between them. Her body molded to his, reminding him of the first time they made love. The ache in his groin increased with the thought of her. God, she felt good in his arms. Kissing her had only let her know he still had feelings for her. The magnetic pull of her sexuality trickled though his veins, rendering him helpless. He slumped in a chair and kicked off his shoes.

"Admit it, after all that happened between you, you still love her." He spoke aloud to the empty room. It was as simple as that. There had never been another woman like her. When they first met, their passion had been so electrifying he was certain it would abate over time. Instead, it had become stronger when they finally made love. It was dynamite.

What the hell was he thinking? No way was it possible, especially now.

His affair with Barbara had come to an end last night. She wanted things he couldn't give her and had found someone who could. It was a relief in a way, especially after running into Nancy again. He had hated her for so long, and now he discovered he still loved her.

He stretched out on his bed to think. Damn, he never expected anything like this to happen. He had planned to tell Nancy just where they stood and leave. Instead, Tom showed up and things got out of hand. Tom had never forgiven him for taking her away from him, but she had never belonged to Tom.

It looked like he was still hanging around, hoping she would change her mind. If she was going to marry Tom, she would have done it years ago. It buoyed his spirits to know she had chosen someone else to marry.

Nancy was ready to throw him out after his insulting remarks. It wasn't like him to say something like that. Her beautiful face kept plaguing him, and he couldn't get her out of his mind. Why shouldn't she have a lover? She was single, smart, and beautiful.

What was happening to make him feel this way after all this time? He was never jealous before. Where did that thought come from? He couldn't seem to do a darn thing to stop what was occurring. He could only keep his distance and try to ignore her. It was going to be a lot easier said than done.

On Monday morning, Mrs. Caulfield, his new secretary, greeted him with a warm smile. "Commander MacLane is waiting in your office."

"Thank you. Rather early isn't he?" Sam looked at his watch.

"The Commander is always up and about this early," she replied, smiling.

"Thank you, Mrs. Caulfield. I'll keep that in mind."

The office looked like any other military office, only larger as befit a Commanding Officer. The furniture was the best and the view terrific. Outside his window, a short distance away, he had a breathtaking view of sand dunes and the sea.

Commander Kevin MacLane, Mac to his friends, was Sam's executive officer. A man he knew to be a friend and an excellent officer. They had served together on the same ship some years ago. Mac would see Sam through the squalls that lay ahead. Some new Commanding Officers went through rough times at the beginning of a new command. That was why they had an Executive Officer and a competent staff to guide them through.

Close to six feet tall, Mac was solidly built with dark hair and alert brown eyes. Most people were intimidated by his stature. Sam knew from previous experience Mac wasn't a man to fool with.

He watched Mac pour coffee into mugs from a white carafe. Smiling, he turned and handed a cup to Sam. He accepted the coffee because he hadn't gotten much sleep last night thinking about Nancy.

With a hefty gulp Sam swallowed the hot brew, feeling its heat warm his insides. "Thanks, I needed this."

"Has it been rough weekend?"

"You don't know the half of it." Sam replied as he sat down at his desk.

Mac sat across from him. "Don't bet on it."

Mac's half smile turned into a knowing grin. Mischief glinted in his dark eyes. He was at the club so he knew the events that took place on Saturday night.

"News travels fast around here, especially when it concerns Lieutenant Smith-Owens." Mac observed.

"Oh? What's so special about Lieutenant Smith-Owens?" Sam leaned back in his chair, waiting.

"You rattled her cage." Mac smiled as if he knew something.

"Is that good or bad?" He spoke with a good-natured grin.

"Lieutenant Smith-Owens is one of the coolest junior officers we have. Very seldom anyone ruffles her feathers. You did a good job of it Saturday night. It's all over the base."

"Great, there is nothing like starting off on the right foot in a new command," Sam answered.

"It'll blow over." Mac said.

"I'm sure it will. Most gossip does." Sam took another swallow of his coffee, savoring its mellow flavor.

"You know the drill."

"Yes." He knew all too well how a simple incident could get blown out of portion. He tried to hide his eagerness for any information about Nancy.

"Scuttlebutt comes and goes," Mac said "I've worked with the Lieutenant since she was assigned to this staff. She can charm the balls off a brass monkey and handles everyone with an ease you wouldn't believe. No one upsets her from Admirals on down. She makes you feel like she's doing you a favor and you're the only one she has to please."

"She sounds too good to be true," Sam remarked. "What's her problem? She must have some faults. Does she drink?" Sam hadn't intended to ask that question because he already knew she couldn't drink, but had forgotten about it.

"Whatever gave you that idea?" Mac looked a little perplexed.

"She evidently wasn't at her best Saturday night," Sam explained.

"From what I saw, it made me wonder. She doesn't drink anything stronger than tonic water with a slice of lime or sometimes cola mixed with orange juice."

"That's an odd mixture." Sam cringed at the thought of what Mac described.

"She seems to like it pretty well. I've tried it, and it's not a bad combination."

Sam was a bourbon and ginger man when he drank. He learned long ago to limit himself to two drinks at all times. "You seem to think highly of her."

"I do. There's no hanky panky. I love my wife, and they happen to be good friends. She often stays with our boys when Stella and I need to get away for a weekend. Her son and our boys get along well together.

"She has a son?" Sam pretended to be surprised. "If she has a son, what's she doing in the Navy?"

"She's from a long line of Naval Officers, and when her brother, Lieutenant Commander Jeremiah Smith, was killed in a crash at sea, she joined up to carry on the family tradition. Her parents take care of her son David, and he attends a military school in the Northwestern part of the state."

Sam moved some papers around on his desk. He hoped Mac didn't notice. Sam had lost a good friend in Jerry and how well he remembered the time spent at the farm and Nancy. At the time, he couldn't do anything to help because he was still in Vietnam fighting a hellish war.

"It isn't like her to be clumsy." Mac looked puzzled over Nancy's behavior.

"The Lieutenant certainly was Saturday night." The thought of holding Nancy for that few minutes reminded him of times past. She was anything but clumsy. She was a tomboy when they met, and she blossomed into a beautiful and vibrant woman.

So Nancy had a friend in Mac. What would Mac do if he knew Sam was the reason for her strange behavior? Seeing her again had upset him more than he wanted to admit, and yesterday's events hadn't helped. Old desires had been awakened, and worst of all, he believed he was still in love with her.

"Every eligible officer, including some of the 'Point's' finest hot shot fly boys, has tried to make time with her. None too successfully, I might add."

"You take quite an interest in the young Lieutenant. How did the man she was with Saturday night make the grade?" Sam tried not to notice Mac's inquiring glance.

"Lieutenant O'Brian and Nancy are just friends. It's strictly that. Nancy keeps him around to ward off all the wolves barking at her door. She's particular about any dates. It's as if she's comparing them with some past lover and none of them match up."

Sam pushed his chair back and stood. He turned toward the window, hoping Mac wouldn't see his face. So Nancy was particular about the men she dated. Was he conceited enough to think she compared her men to him? Why would she? He would be seeing her practically every day, and it would be difficult to apologize for his behavior Saturday night and yesterday, but he'd have to find a way to do it.

He turned back to Mac. "Okay, you've got my interest, tell me the rest."

"Most of the time, she's calm, cool, and collected. She's a good worker and doesn't shirk her duties, but lately something has been bothering her, and dammed if I know what it is. It must be something personal because she's put papers in to resign her commission."

"She has?" Sam rubbed his hand across his face as though he was tired. "I'm sorry to hear that since you claim she's a good officer."

"Whatever her problem is, it's deep and personal, and she's not talking. She hasn't confided in me or Stella about the real reason for her resignation. I kind of mislaid her papers, hoping she would change her mind and tell me why."

"If the Lieutenant is unhappy for some reason, put her papers through and I'll sign them." He didn't have to guess the reason for Nancy's decision. He already knew it.

"Senator Tom Brewster has offered her a job, but, I don't think she'll accept it. She's not into politics."

"Senator Brewster? She's aiming high." Sam tried to keep his voice on an even keel and act as if he didn't know the Senator. Maybe Tom was finally winning Nancy over, but he doubted it after yesterday.

Mac broke into Sam's thoughts. "They've been friends for years, and the Senator has been trying for some time to get her to work for him, but she's hesitant."

"Maybe she has her reasons." Last night, Nancy didn't act like a person even remotely interested in Tom. She acted indifferent toward him.

He suspected she probably figured it would cause him some embarrassment if the word of their affair was made public even though it happened years ago. Could there be another reason he didn't know about?

He felt restless. For a long time, he stood with his hands folded behind his back, staring out the window at the huge expanse of dark blue-green water and the dunes. He didn't know what to think.

"Is something wrong, sir?"

"No, I'm just overtired."

Still, his thoughts wandered. He had hurt Nancy by accusing her of being drunk at the club. Then yesterday, a streak of jealousy had reared its ugly head when he couldn't help overhearing the calls she received. Why the hell hadn't he kept his mouth shut? He wanted to strike back at her and hurt her as she had hurt him.

Now he was sure she was resigning her commission to protect him. Damn, what a mess. How the devil was he going to right the mistakes he'd made? Did he want to do that? Life was getting too damn complicated. Sam brooded, but no answers appeared.

Mac interrupted his thoughts. "Lieutenant Kelly Thurston is also on staff. Watch out for her. She's always on the prowl and that's how she got the nickname Thursty. She'll give you more trouble than the whole staff will."

"In what way?" Sam prompted.

"She's blonde, beautiful, and smart. She thinks her good looks will get her everything she wants, and she uses them to charm and snare any available men."

"What does she want besides a man?"

"She's interested in money, prestige, and a handsome Senior Officer."

"She picked the wrong place to find the first two." Sam turned to look and Mac for a minute. "As for the third, most senior officers are either married or old."

"You're not, and it doesn't matter to Thursty. She's hard to figure out at times. When I think I have her pegged, she does an about face. She's self-centered and jealous of Lieutenant Smith-Owens. Lately, she's been acting like the cat that swallowed the canary. She's been easier to be around this last month or so."

"Maybe she's found what she's looking for," Sam suggested.

"Could be. If she has, she's being very secretive about her latest conquest, otherwise you would hear all about it."

"So, two of my principle Lieutenants don't get along. That's all I need. It's a heck of a way to start a new job."

"It'll get better." Mac assured him.

"Will it?" Sam wasn't so sure.

* * * *

The first weeks proceeded with all the snafus that could possibly happen. If what Mac said was true about Lieutenant Thurston having a lover, it didn't seem to stop her from making subtle advances toward him.

She lost little time in letting him know she was available. It didn't seem to bother her that he was her commanding officer. Having Nancy around, only made things more difficult.

Thursty was beautiful, voluptuous, and knew how to attract a man's attention in not so subtle ways. If Sam saw her once, he saw her at least ten times a day. She consulted him about every little problem she could have easily taken care of herself or asked Nancy.

He made sure his office door was open at all times so Mrs. Caulfield could hear all of the conversations in his office with his female officers. Finding a way to inform Thursty he wasn't interested took all the skill of a politician, especially with all the harassment charges being hurled at some of his fellow officers. The frosting on top of the cake looked sweet, but wasn't. Besides, he liked to pick his own desserts.

Nancy was a different story. She only saw him when it pertained to some business Mac needed resolved. All transactions were strictly professional, and he maintained a cool demeanor whenever they were together. Yet, he could feel her reserve melt away, little by little. No reference was ever made to the past and what happened that weekend at her place. There were many times he caught himself thinking of her and wished she would come to him with some problem. She came infrequently. Mac had been right. She was efficient and work oriented.

In his quarters, a night didn't pass that he slept without thinking about Nancy. She turned his feelings inside out. He would have to do something to stop it and soon. Thank goodness, Beth, his daughter, and Mrs. Doyle, his housekeeper, arrived this weekend.

* * * *

The events of the past weeks had taken their toll on Nancy. The more she was around Sam, the more mixed her feelings grew. Everything between them was strictly above board. No intimate conversations or looks passed between them. It was strictly, 'Yes, sir' and 'No, sir'. Her nerves were raw, and she looked forward to the weekend.

Nancy had promised David she would be home. She also wanted to talk to her father about her sister and the allegations Tom had made. For someone who was organized, her thoughts went in all directions. She couldn't concentrate on her work and didn't know which way to turn.

Chapter Twenty

The beautiful weather and the drive to Smithfield helped Nancy clear her head. The farmhouse was her retreat away from all the worries and petty problems at work that had occurred in the last few weeks. It had been two weeks since Tom had dropped his bombshell insinuating Rita might be the source of her problems.

Her father, Edward, was waiting for her as she drove into the driveway, parked the car, and joined him. He came forward with his arms outstretched and wrapped her in his arms. He hugged her tight. Ruth joined them.

"Did you have a busy month?" he said as she moved away from him.

"Yes, and a lot of unforeseen developments at work."

Nancy hugged Ruth. Her eyes searched the yard for David.

Before she could ask where he was, her father spoke. "David's gone fishing with the Mason boys."

"The Mason boys?" For a moment, she drew a blank and then remembered.

"Stop worrying, he's fine. The older boy, Terry, watches out for him."

"I always worry." She was trying not to show a mother's concern.

"I know that look," Edward said. "There's something else bothering you. Is something wrong at work, and do you want to talk about it now or later?"

"Now is as good a time as any. Then I can enjoy the rest of the weekend."

Edward sat in one of the comfortable chairs on the screened porch.

"Make yourselves comfortable while I get some lemonade," Ruth advised. "It's going to be another hot one. I'm glad you're staying for the weekend, dear." Ruth's warm welcome lightened her mood.

"Yes, if I'm not in the way."

"You're never in the way," Ruth said over her shoulder as she entered the main house.

Nancy paced the floor instead of sitting in a chair. She had no idea how to start.

Her father interrupted her pacing. "Something pretty important has happened to upset you this way. Are you going to tell me, or are you going to keep me waiting while you wear out the porch floor?"

"I need to talk to someone before I go crazy." Then she blurted it out. "Sam is my new commanding officer."

"Sam? Sam Arlington?" A look of disbelief showed on her father's aging face.

"Remember? I mentioned we were expecting a new Commanding Officer. The Captain who was to take over had a severe heart attack and Sam came in as his replacement."

"I see your predicament." He rubbed his clean-shaven chin.

"If I tried to miss the change of Command Ceremonies a lot of questions would have been asked. I had to be there."

"What happened?"

"He recognized me. It was a tense moment for both of us. He asked a few questions and passed on. I don't think anybody suspected we knew each other, except..." Nancy hesitated.

"Except who?"

"Commander MacLane and Lieutenant Thurston are the only two who are suspicious."

"I don't think Mac will cause you any problems."

"I saw Sam at the reception after the inspection and again on Saturday night at the Officer's Club. I was with Mike and had just gotten my food from the Buffet table when someone bumped my arm and my food went flying all over Sam's sport jacket, He wasn't too happy about it. Then I bumped into him on the way from the ladies room. The hall was dark and my heel broke. I landed in his arms. It didn't help, and he insinuated I was drunk. He called me on Sunday, and I told him I didn't want to see him, but he came by the house anyway."

"Did the two of you get matters straightened out?"

"I told him politely and firmly I didn't want him back in my life again."

"What did he say to that?"

"He said the feeling was mutual, and he didn't want me back in his life either after what I had done to him."

"What had you done?" Her father looked puzzled.

"He said I stopped writing and never gave him any explanation. I told him I never received any letters from him and there were no answers to my letters either."

"You did answer his letters," her father said. "I remember you writing to him every time I turned around. Maybe the war had something to do with his not getting your mail, but he should have received a few of them."

"He insisted he never received any mail from me, but he received a few letters from Rita. He doesn't believe I wrote to him."

"Both of you wrote, yet neither of you received the other's mail. Yet he received some from Rita. Even in a war, some mail gets through and why did he get hers and not any of yours?" A frown covered her father's face.

"Why are you frowning?" She wondered if he thought about Rita as the cause.

"Nothing's the matter."

"Tom showed up. Of course, he and Sam never got along. It was like keeping two tigers at bay. The animosity between them was palatable. It seems Tom had something to do with Sam being billeted overseas for so long. He had the power and used it to keep us apart."

"Yes, I can see Tom using his influence to get what he wanted and that was you. It didn't work because you were in love with Sam."

"After Sam left, Tom mentioned Rita might have been the one who took my letters and that she still wanted Sam."

Nancy paced the floor and stopped to look at her father. An absent-minded look showed on his face.

"I wished I'd paid more attention." He appeared thoughtful.

"What are you saying?"

"Rita insisted on taking the mail to the box and picking it up. It was something to keep her busy."

"I know she disliked me, but do you don't think she would stoop so low as to deprive David from knowing his father."

"If she was in one of her many depressive moods, I wouldn't put it past her. She's always been jealous of you, and she has never pretended any love for David."

Nancy wanted to deny it. "Rita would never do anything like that. She's my sister."

"You never know. You better confront her when you see her and hear what she has to say. She's become so unpredictable, more so than in the past. She's giving everyone a hard time, even Joe. You know they separated, and still she taunts him. We've had to hire special nurses to take care of her. She's self destructive."

"Joe has been so good to her all these years. I'm surprised he stayed around this long."

"I think he's at the end of his rope, trying to help her when she doesn't want anyone's help."

"He loves her."

"Sometime love isn't enough. Joe's afraid she might do herself bodily harm with the depression, the pills, and the booze." Her father turned his palms up in a gesture of defeat.

"She's drinking again?"

"Yes, we don't know where she gets it. Her behavior changes just after a visit from Tom. I've asked him to stay away. The next step is the hospital."

"She'd kill herself before she'd let that happen."

"It's possible she's already trying to do that. Sometimes she mixes her pills with whiskey and forgets she takes them. Your sister can be crafty at times. I presume you haven't had time to tell Sam about David."

"All he knows is that I have a son. He was married, his wife died, and he has a daughter two years younger than David. From what gossips claim, he's about to marry, but he denied it."

"That's not good, but I've never known Sam to lie." Her father sighed.

"He didn't act like someone in love and said the lady in question was in love with someone else."

"Then there's still hope."

"Hope? Dad, you're a total romantic. Not all love affairs have a happy ending."

"Most of them do." His endearing smile disarmed her.

"I'm resigning my commission." She slipped that bit of information in hoping her father wouldn't notice.

"You're what?" His voice rose an octave or two. He looked shocked.

"It's the only way I see out of this mess without hurting Sam."

"You won't accept Tom's offer, will you?" A worried look crossed his face.

"No, I have the feeling he's not interested in me any more. He hardly calls, and when he does, he's not pressing me to take his job offer. I think he's finally found someone."

"Let's hope so. I like Tom, but haven't been happy with his ideas and have stopped backing him."

"I'm glad."

"Let's change the subject. Are you still interested in Holly House? It's come up for sale."

"Oh, definitely. I've wanted to buy a house for David and me."

"Good, I brought it and signed the papers this morning. It's now yours. When you have time, you can start working on the house to get it in shape. In the meantime, I've hired a crew to bring the gardens back to their original beauty. It's our gift to you and David for all the love and happiness you've given us."

"That's wonderful, Dad, but what will Rita say?"

"Rita wanted the cottage, and we gave it to her. Now this is our gift to you and David."

Nancy nodded, pleased at his thoughtfulness. "Let's get back to Sam. I don't intend telling Sam about David for a while. I can't very well go up to him and say 'Oh, by the way, Captain, remember that affair we had years ago. Just after you left I found out I was pregnant and bore you a son.' Not likely, after he insulted me the way he did." She told her dad about Saturday night.

"He did what?" Her father looked angry now. "I don't believe Sam would do that."

"Sunday, while Sam was at the house, David called. I didn't want Sam to know who it was and pretended he was a boyfriend. Then Tom called and I let it ring. You know Tom. His recorded message came over loud and clear. It gave Sam the impression I had several boy friends, and I was sleeping with all of them. Sam got mad."

"He's jealous."

"No way." She considered it possible, but she preferred to believe otherwise. "Tom came by while Sam was there and things got a little wild. Tom hinted to Sam that he reminded him of someone he knew, referring to David. The only thing I could think of to distract Tom was to stumble and fall against Sam."

"Did it help?" Her father wore an amused smile.

"No, it made things worse. It was so unexpected. Sam lost his balance and fell backwards onto the couch pulling me down with him. I ended up sprawled over him, and he held on to me and wouldn't let go. I didn't want him to let go."

"Oh, I see." An amused gleam in sparkled in his eye.

"All the old feelings came swimming back. It was if he was telling Tom, 'she's mine and don't even think you have a chance, because you don't.' Dad, what am I going to do?"

"What was Tom doing all this time?"

"Watching and evaluating the situation to see how he could use it to his advantage."

"That's Tom. You've known him all your life, but be careful. As you already know, he doesn't like to take no for an answer, and he hates to lose."

"Don't I know it. He has many secrets. He's acting different, as though he doesn't want anyone to know what he's up to. He warned me to watch my step."

"That's strange. Is it because of Sam?"

"I think he wants to see Sam disgraced in some way."

"Maybe it was just a friendly warning."

"He said it in a nice way, and then he tried to blackmail me over my affair with Sam. You remember Mom taught us how to write down every day's events and keep them in a diary. I'm glad I still do. He didn't like it when I told him to stay away from Sam and that two could play his game."

"I take it your dairy has some revealing information about Tom that he wouldn't like revealed to the public."

"Yes. It's locked away in a safe place and will stay there unless I really have a use for it."

"Smart girl, Sharon taught you well."

"With his pull in high places, he managed to keep Sam billeted overseas and away from me. Let's hope he's met someone he really likes and that she is as sly and as nasty as he is so he'll leave me alone."

"I see, you still have some feelings for Sam."

"Dad, I'm so confused when he's around. I'm all tingly and excited. When he's not near, I miss him and wish he was with me. What if he doesn't feel the same way? I don't know what I would do."

"Don't you think it would be better to tell him about David than have him find out from someone else like Tom or Rita?"

"Yes, but I've got to find the right time."

"You have two men to contend with. Both are powerful in their own right. With Tom's innuendoes, you don't have much leeway."

"I know." She expelled a deep breath.

"Sam may use some of his power against you if you step out of line, but I doubt it. I have never taken him for that kind of man. Tom's a different story. He's a politician through and through and knows his way around. He's waited a long time for you. Even though you've told him many times you're not interested, he still wants you any way he can get you. Just hope he's met someone more pliable and thinks the way he does." Her father looked pensive. "So Sam is still number one?"

"I wish I could say no, but I've always loved Sam. Even after I learned I was pregnant and didn't hear from him. I hated him for a while, but then there was David. I could never hate him after that."

Her father came over and hugged her. "Baby, this is your father you're talking to. It isn't wrong to have feelings for the man you once loved and still do. He is the father of your child. I just don't want you hurt again."

"Dad, I thought I was through loving him. Now he's back in my life, and I'm thoroughly confused."

The kitchen door swung open and Ruth entered carrying a tray of ice-cold lemonade she set next to them and returned to the kitchen without interrupting them.

"You're just like your mother. You can only truly love one man." He rested her head against his shoulder.

"What am I to do?"

"Take one day at a time. Your problems will disappear."

"What Sam thinks of me shouldn't matter, but it does. If he learns about David, he might think I'm an unfit mother and try to take him away."

"You're a very good mother. Sam is the type of man who would be proud to know he has a son like David."

"He's a captain, wanting to make Rear Admiral. You know what a scandal would do to his career."

"Do we? Times have changed, and this all happened before your career in the Navy. Knowing he has a son will outweigh all other considerations. Only a few people know about your affair with Sam."

He sipped a glass of lemonade. "You resigned your commission when you learned Sam was coming so not to embarrass him. Not every woman would give up her career for the man she loved.

"You have enough money from Roger's estate to last you and David a long time. Tom may know all about you and Sam, but he would only hurt himself if he tried to use it against you." Nancy nodded her agreement

"He's a brilliant Senator," her father continued, "and needs to know all about the people that work for him. I don't think he would jeopardize his future by using unethical means to hurt you. You'll be a civilian in a few weeks. Maybe the lid will stay on your secret till then, and it won't matter what happens."

Chapter Twenty-one

The farmhouse's back door opened and slammed shut with a loud thud. The voices of three young boys intermingled with Gypsy's gleeful yapping. Her father's consternation turned into a smile when he heard the commotion. The noise ended their conversation.

Nancy and her father hurried to the kitchen to meet the invaders. Ruth was preparing sandwiches for them. The three boys stood bedraggled and dirty. Their morning's catch wiggled in a pail of water by the kitchen door. Nancy watched her son with a pride only a mother could feel.

David saw her. "Hey, Mom," he hollered. "When did you get home?"

"A little while ago."

An affectionate hug and kiss from her son sent warm shivers through Nancy. When he pulled away, he looked up at her with shining brown eyes. He had his father's eyes and reassuring smile. Her heart squeezed with pain. What if Sam didn't want him? The thought sent chills through her.

"What's the matter, Mom? You look scared." Nancy looked towards her father for his reassuring smile.

"I'm fine, it's just that you're growing like a weed and getting handsomer every time I see you." Lost in her tumultuous thoughts, she couldn't think straight. She would have to do as her father said, and take one day at a time.

The Mason boys stayed for lunch, and afterwards they played touch football. It was early in the afternoon when they left, leaving Nancy with thoughts she didn't want.

After seeing his friends off, David came running back into the house and hugged her. Gypsy was trailing behind him looking for his share of love.

"Can we go for a walk, Mom?"

"Sure, where do you want to go?"

"To sit on the swing under the willows."

They left the house with Gypsy bounding back and forth across their path. A stirring breeze blew in from the river to rattle the leaves like old bones. The ferry's whistle echoed through the afternoon's stillness.

"Are you all right, Mom?" David had a frown on his face.

"I'm fine, darling." She warned herself to smile in reassurance.

They sat under the willows for a long time and watched the boats on the river. David laid his head in her lap, and she leaned back against the seat to doze. A while later when she woke, David sat up.

With his strong young hands, he brushed a lock of her hair back from her face. "Something's bugging you. Are you going to tell me what?"

"You're getting to be just like your grandfather, thinking you can spot my moods." Her laugh was light and gay.

"Something is wrong. You're far away."

"Am I?"

"Yes, you are. Tell to me."

"This was my favorite spot, and it was here when your father first kissed me."

"Do you still love him?"

"Sometimes, I'm angry for his going away and not coming back to us. Other times, I don't know." She said nothing more a moment. "Yes, there are times when I find myself still loving him."

"Tell me about him. You never say much."

The willows swayed to the river breeze, and a chill touched her. "I've told you a hundred times about him. After our first meeting, he thought I was too young and a tomboy. He wasn't interested." She smiled, remembering Sam. "Then he learned differently."

"Is that when he started calling you his Elegant Swan?"

"Yes. He said I reminded him of the swans he saw in the lakes in

Europe and thought the name fit me."

"You're like one. I know about the tomboy part, especially when you get with the kids and play ball. Even Grandma Ruth says you're like a chameleon and can fit in anywhere."

"She does, does she?"

"Why can't Aunt Rita be like you, always happy and smiling? You'd think after she married Mr. Hoskins she'd have been happy, but she isn't. He built her that nice big house farther up the river. Now, she's acting funny again. Grandpa says to stay away from her."

"Your aunt has a sickness she can't control, even with medication."

"Grandpa and Grandma Ruth talked one night. They don't like her coming over to visit anymore."

"Your Aunt Rita has been that way for as long as I can remember. It's as though she's s afraid to be happy, and yet she resents anyone else who is."

Nancy turned away, hoping to keep her wayward tears in check. She and Rita had never gotten along. It was a shame that a woman with everything was so mean and unhappy that even a child like David noticed.

"Mom, please tell me what's wrong. We've never hidden things from each other."

She wiped her eyes on the sleeve of her shirt and pulled David close. "A lot of things are happening, and I've come to a big decision."

"What kind of decision?"

"I'm leaving the Navy."

"Oh. You're not going to work for Senator Brewster. No way. I don't like him."

"I didn't know you felt that strongly about it. I have no intention of taking the job with Tom."

"Then why are you resigning your commission? You love the Navy."

"There comes a time in everyone's life when they learn there are other paths in life they need to explore. I think the time has come for me."

"The way you've acted lately, I knew something was wrong. Just promise me one thing. You won't work for the Senator."

"You've already made it clear you don't want me working for Tom. You've never been crazy about him and neither have I."

"He's all right, but he never has time to do fun things. All he does is run to meetings and talk on the phone about politics."

"Suppose I take some time off before looking for a job? Grandpa bought us a house."

"He has?" David smiled, a big one.

"Yes, Holly House over on Berry Lane I've always liked the house, and now it's ours."

"You'll have your own room."

"Can I decorate it the way I want?"

"Yes. I presume it will include anything to do with ships and planes."

"You know it. I'll carry on the family tradition."

"Darling, it would make us all very happy, especially Grandpa. Next time I'm home, we'll go over and see what has to be done to get the house in order. Just be patient."

"Mom, did Grandpa really buy it for us?"

"Yes." She hugged him and held him for a long time. Looking over his shoulder, all she could think of was Sam. She thought it best not to mention his father yet.

His I.D. bracelet caught in her hair and fell. It landed on the ground. She bent over and picked it up. The warm gold slid through her hands.

"You're still wearing your father's bracelet."

"Mom, it's the only thing I have of his."

"Yes, I know." She sighed, trying not to let the past intrude on the little time they had together.

"I'm glad he had trouble with the clasp and had to leave before you could take it back from the jeweler. I still have trouble with it. I'll take it to the jewelers when I go back to school."

Nancy felt the gold with the Navy seal on it and turned it over to read the inscription, 'To Sam, with all my love, Nancy.' She had been so young, so in love, and she was afraid to admit she still was.

The future she had been so sure of a few weeks ago had blown up in her face with his arrival. Her son was growing up, and the thought of sharing him with his father scared her.

She let her thoughts drift away from Sam and thought about confronting Rita over the letters.

Chapter Twenty-two

Sam had little time to think of Barbara and her departure. It was just as well they called it quits.

A cold shower did little to lessen the feeling of heavy seas pulling him under. Scuttlebutt about what happened at the Officer's club with Nancy died a slow death.

Late one Friday night, after everyone one left and he sat engrossed in what he was doing. His back bothered from sitting too long, and he stretched to get the kinks out.

Kneading hands sneaked around his shoulders and lower. He looked up to see Lieutenant Thurston. She was still trying her best to put him in a comprising position. Yesterday, at every move he made, she zeroed in on him. Tonight she was wore a tight fitting skirt and a bare off the shoulder midriff top.

"Now isn't that soothing," she cooed.

"Lieutenant Thurston what the devil do you think you're doing? You're not in uniform and have no business here at this time of night." He didn't wait for an answer as he scrambled out of his chair.

"Keep your hands to yourself if you want to keep your job."

"You looked like you were enjoying it," she said in a sultry voice.

"Your conduct is inappropriate for a naval officer. Get out of my office and stay out."

He was tired and aggravated. Lieutenant Thurston was out of order and annoying the hell out of him. He'd see she was transferred out of his command. If it had been Nancy, he might have relaxed and enjoyed the back rub. She always knew the exact spots to rub. Oh hell, he was thinking of her again.

He wondered if his latest rejection of Lieutenant Thurston's numerous invitations deterred her. She was a determined woman who didn't like rejection. The time before this, he'd been sitting at his desk when Lieutenant Thurston, dreamy eyed, leaned over his shoulder and put her mouth close to his ear and whispered 'I'm available,' as though they were lovers.

Then, the phone rang. He picked up the phone and answered. "This is Captain Arlington, speaking."

"I thought you might need rescuing." He recognized Nancy's low seductive voice.

"Thanks for reminding me about dinner, Mac. It'll take me about ten-minutes to get there." He put the phone down and looked up at Lieutenant Thurston. He hadn't forgotten what she tried to do.

"Don't try that maneuver again." The tone of his voice told her to be careful or she'd find herself out the door.

"Now, get out."

With a satisfied smile on her face, she turned, and left his office. She wasn't upset at his refusal and his reprimand.

Maybe Lieutenant Thurston had found someone else to bait, or had she finally taken his warning seriously. She had never tried to get him in a compromising situation until tonight.

In the next weeks, she walked around with a smug look on her face and was nice to everyone. She acted like a cat who had a mouse cornered and was going in for the kill. He wondered who the poor sucker was?

Since his arrival, the tension between his two Lieutenants was stretched to the limit. Now, Lieutenant Thurston was friendly with everyone including Nancy. She was up to something, and he wished he knew what.

A few days later, Mac knocked on his door and entered. He closed the door behind him, something he never did.

"I need to talk to you about Lieutenant Thurston." Mac looked serious.

"What is she up to now, other than trying to corner me in a comprising situation?" Sam released a big sigh.

"I put in the papers to have her transferred like you asked, and they were denied. I did a little digging and talked to a friend of mine at the Pentagon and learned that anything pertaining to Lieutenant Thurston was to be funneled through Senator Tom Brewster on the QT."

"Well I'll be damned." He should have guessed. "She's snagged herself a Senator. So that's why she's been so nice lately. She's found a bigger fish to fry."

If Thursty had caught the Senator's eye, it opened up possibilities. Maybe he'd leave Nancy alone, but did Nancy know or care?

The following weeks Sam found the workload staggering and, for now, he worked long hours trying to get things in order. His personal life had him worrying about more important things than Lieutenant Thurston and Senator Tom Brewster.

The department picnic on Saturday was an opportunity for the staff to let off steam. Mrs. Doyle had arrived and it would give Beth a chance to attend and meet some young people. Mac had mentioned Nancy and her son would be there with his family. It was a way to see her without all the restraints of command between them, and he was looking forward to it. He would make his token appearance and then leave so everyone could enjoy themselves without the old man around.

* * * *

Nancy found her life growing complicated, but stayed out of Sam's way at work. Often she found herself in his company. When she was alone with him, she kept her professional persona and didn't stick around when her business was finished.

It wasn't like Tom to stay way and not call. She hoped he'd met someone else and kept too busy impressing his new love. The situation with her sister Rita worried her. The last time she was home, Rita was nowhere to be found. She was more concerned about her sister then she wanted to admit. Especially after her father told her Rita had slipped into her old habits again.

What free time she had she spent at the farm and Holly House. Her father had some repairmen get the house in shape for her and David. He was coming in for the weekend to attend the department picnic on Saturday. She could relax because Sam would probably make a token appearance and leave. She heard his daughter and housekeeper had arrived the week before and wondered what the girl would be like.

A lot of questions ran through her mind about their lost letters, her sister, and Sam. It was better to stop anticipating and let things take their natural course, but she couldn't stop thinking about them. Had she done the right thing by not telling David about his father and his half sister? Sam was bound to show up at the picnic with his daughter. There was no way they could avoid meeting them. David would treat the girl like he treated the MacLanes' daughter, Jordan, with kindness.

* * * *

Saturday morning started off cool and sunny. As the day advanced, the weather became hotter, but everyone still enjoyed themselves. For today, rank and office politics were forgotten.

Mac, Stella, and their children were sitting with a little girl she didn't recognize. Nancy knew immediately who she was with her dark curly hair and bright smile, the spitting image of Sam.

"Hey Nancy, David," Mac's wife Stella called out." Haven't seen you in awhile. Come sit with us. How have you been?" Small boned and thin, Stella's dark hair and eyes reflected her Spanish ancestry.

"Hi, everyone." Nancy added a big smile to her greeting.

Mac nodded and moved over so she could sit next to Stella. David sat down in front with the boys.

"This is Beth, Captain Arlington's daughter, and this is Lieutenant Smith-Owens and her son David."

"It's nice to meet you Lieutenant Smith-Owens and David."

"How do you like it here?" Nancy said to make conversation, hoping not to make the child feel nervous at meeting someone new.

"It's good to be settled. I'm sure we'll enjoy our stay here."

The girl acted more grownup than most kids her age. Military children grew up fast.

Other friends came and greeted them. Jordan and Beth ran off to play. After chatting with Stella for a while, Nancy left to mingle and greet other friends. She came back to sit with Stella and watched the kids chase each other. Jordan and Beth had joined the boys in the games.

A short distance away, she glimpsed Sam dressed in dungarees and a matching sport shirt. He had a soda in his hands and was talking to

Mac. Their conversation was lost in all the noise floating around her from the crowd of people.

"We haven't seen you much lately," Stella said.

"I've been keeping pretty busy. My parents brought me an old farmhouse close to them, and I'm spending my weekends working on it, bringing it up to date."

"Mac mentioned you'd put in your resignation. What made you do it?" A worried look showed on her face.

"I've thought about it for some time." Her voice was as normal as she could make it.

"Did Senator Brewster finally win you over?"

"His job offer is a great opportunity, but it's not for me." What did she really want now that Sam had reentered her life?

It seemed the harder they tried to avoid each other, the more they bumped into one another. The longing and the need for him strengthened. Maybe resigning was the answer, and if it wasn't, she really lost nothing. Her experience in the Navy would help her land a good job no matter what she chose to do.

"Nancy, snap out of it, you're miles away."

"Sorry, what's happening?"

David came running up with Beth in tow. He was all smiles. "I won this for Beth."

"Isn't it lovely?" Beth beamed at David, hugging a stuffed tiger with its black stripes and gold fur, with a red velvet tongue and black eyes.

"He sure is a beauty. Have you found a name for it?"

"Not yet," Beth said. "But David and I will think of one."

Before Nancy could say anymore they ran off to show Sam. She noticed Beth had somehow attached herself to David and was introducing him to her father. Sam sent a fleeting look Nancy's way. She shivered, hoping Stella didn't notice.

Stella's children swarmed around them telling them about the games they had entered and showed the prizes they had won. David came running back to her, asking if it was all right for him to join in the softball game. Each team was to be divided between grownups and kids so the scoring wouldn't be lopsided. Some played with their fathers and others played against their dads. Thank goodness, Sam and David were on opposite teams.

The game was exciting as Nancy watched the kids slide into the bases as though they were fighting for their lives. Their mothers cheered from the bleachers.

The score was tied six to six when David slid into third base and into Sam, who was coaching. Sam helped him up. David brushed off his clothes and looked around as though he lost something.

"My God, he's lost his bracelet." She looked around to see if anyone heard her. With all the noise, no one had noticed her outburst.

Nancy watched Sam bend down and pick up the bracelet from the dirt and hand it to David. From this distance, she couldn't tell anything by the look on Sam face. Some people got boisterous around them so Nancy couldn't see with all the people jumping up and down. Impulsively, she grabbed hold of Stella's arm.

"Nancy what's the matter?"

"I'm sorry. I felt dizzy for a moment. I guess the heat is getting to me. I'll be all right." Her insides roiled at the thought of Sam seeing his bracelet after all these years.

"Are you sure? This heat is murder." Stella patted her arm.

The inning ended, and the men came off the field. When she looked up, she saw Sam looking their way with an unhappy look on his face. Nancy reached down for her water bottle and took a swig. Thank goodness the game had resumed and David's team won by two runs.

After the picnic ended and they were on their way to the Navy exchange, Nancy spoke to David.

"Why did you wear your father's bracelet today when you knew the clap wouldn't stay closed?"

"Mom, it's all right. The Captain just picked it up and handed it to me."

"Are you sure?" For all she knew Sam might not have paid any attention to the bracelet, but she thought she saw him turn it over and glance at the back of it.

"I'm positive, Mom. You've never acted this way before. If the Captain's being here upsets you that much, it's a good thing you're getting out."

"What gave you the idea it's the Captain that's bothering me?"

"You've never acted this way about another officer before, so I presumed he was the reason."

"I just have lots on my mind right now with the new house and retiring." She didn't want to fib to David about Sam. "Okay, darling?"

"Sure."

* * * *

David wouldn't tell his mother what the Captain said about having a bracelet similar to his at one time. He'd seen a picture of a man who looked like the Captain in his younger days in his mother's lock box with her diaries. She didn't know he's seen it. It was his secret. David suspected there was something more to his mother's sudden decision to end her Naval career, but he wasn't going to mention it.

He thought he had better change the subject. He liked Beth and thought she might be a good subject to talk about.

"Beth seems to be a nice kid, a little lonely, but I know how that is, being an only child."

"Why, David, you've never mentioned to me about being lonely."

"There are times. I know at times you're lonely, too."

"That's true. What's so urgent that you want to go to the exchange today?"

"I want to buy you a birthday present. I won't be here next week."

"You don't have to spend your allowance on a gift for me."

"I know, but I saw something I knew you'd like when I was here the last time and hope they still have it."

Once inside the Navy exchange, she stopped. "How much time do you want?"

"A half hour should do it. I'll meet you in the food court at my favorite place just in case it takes less time. I'm hungry." He rubbed his stomach.

"You're forever hungry." Mom grinned at him.

David walked off, knowing his mother was watching. He knew she worried about him, especially about not having a father. Mom and his grandparents gave him all the love any boy could want. He was growing tall and another three birthdays he would be thirteen and a teenager. His life would change again and maybe even before that if he was thinking

138

along the right track.

He found his way to the China and Crystal department where he saw the cut glass figurines on display. The small glass swan sat in the foreground on the top shelf of the display case. He approached a salesperson.

"Would you please show me that small glass swan on the top shelf?"

The girl smiled at him. "Are you sure you want to see it? It's quite expensive."

The clerk looked at him and saw he was serious. She took it out of the locked case and set it on a piece of velvet on top of the counter. David admired it.

"I'll take it." He was reaching for his billfold when a girl's voice interrupted him.

"What a lovely swan, David."

He recognized her voice right away and looked to see Beth standing close by with her father.

"Hi, Beth, it's nice to see you again and you too, sir." He hadn't expected to meet anyone, especially the Captain and Beth.

"Good afternoon, David," Sam saw the swan. "Some lucky person was going to get a lovely gift."

"It's a birthday gift for my mother. My dad always said she looked like an elegant swan. I thought this would make a nice present for her." Before David could see the Captain's reaction, the sales clerk drew his attention back to his purchase, and he missed seeing the look on Captain Arlington's face.

* * * *

Sam looked at the boy and couldn't believe what he heard. It felt like a ten-ton truck hit him head on. He remembered the bracelet on the ball field and thought nothing of it, but the swan... He couldn't believe it. There was only one sure way to find out.

"Beth, we have to hurry." Sam said. "I've got to go back to the office, and Mrs. Doyle will be waiting for us. I'm sure David has other things to do."

"But, Daddy, you never mentioned having to go back to work." She pouted.

"Darling, I just remembered there's something I forgot to do. I'll make it up to you, I promise." Sam couldn't wait to get to his office.

"I guess we have to go." Her lip curled down in disappointment. "See you around," she said to David.

"See you around," David repeated and watched them go. He liked Beth. Maybe he'd see her again.

He wondered what made the Captain so uneasy all of a sudden and smiled knowingly. He took his gift and went to meet his mother.

* * * *

Sam thought nothing else could possibly go wrong. Was he mistaken to think David was his son? There was only one way to find out. He had to be sure before he faced Nancy.

He dropped Beth off at home, left her in the capable hands of Mrs. Doyle, and headed for his office. He signed in with the watch. Upstairs, he turned on the lights as he went. He stopped long enough on his way to take Lieutenant Smith-Owens file jacket from the files and into his office. Turning on the lights, he sat down at his desk and looked through Nancy's file.

The date of David's birth registered in his tired mind like a warning light. Nancy must have been pregnant when he left. Why hadn't she mentioned it? Maybe she hadn't known and hadn't wanted to say anything until she was she knew for sure. David was born eight months later so why hadn't she told him then? Think man, it's possible she didn't even know she was pregnant.

Sam looked down at the dates again and knew beyond a doubt that David was his son. He closed Nancy's jacket, put it back in the file, and left the office, perturbed and excited to know he had a son.

Chapter Twenty-three

Sam planned to confront Nancy about David. It wasn't going to be easy. The shock of discovering he had a son was beginning to wear off. Nancy's file, the bracelet, and then David quoting his father. He couldn't be mistaken. First though, he had to go home to Beth. She would be waiting for him. At home, already in her pajamas, Beth greeted him enthusiastically.

"Daddy, I thought you weren't coming home."

"She's been fidgeting and waiting for you," Mrs. Doyle said.

"Come on, pumpkin. Do you think I'd miss putting a pretty young lady like you to bed?"

Beth hugged and kissed him. She took his hand and dragged him behind her up the stairs to her bedroom. She crawled under the covers and lifted her arms to him for another hug.

"Daddy, I love you." Those three words filled his heart.

"I love you more than anything in this world." He responded, tucking her in.

"Even better then Barbara?"

"I don't think you have to worry about her being part of our lives any longer. She's found somebody new."

"I'm glad. Are you unhappy?"

"No, I thought you liked Barbara."

"She's okay, but she'd never make a good Navy wife."

Sam stared at his daughter in amazement. How could one so young be so smart?

"I liked that boy we met today."

Her words stunned him. "You met several boys today."

"The cute one in the exchange," she said shyly.

"You mean, David?" So, his daughter noticed David, too.

"If I had a brother, I would like him to be like David. He didn't ignore me like some of the other kids did."

Beth's remarks surprised the hell out of him. When the time came how was he going to explain David was her half-brother? The brother she had always wanted. Now wasn't the time to worry about that. He had to see Nancy first.

"Do you want me to read to you?"

"Not tonight," she replied in a sleepy voice.

Her eyes were already closed when he kissed her goodnight lightly on the cheek and pushed a lock of her hair out of her face.

He stood outside her door for a few minutes, watching her sleep and deciding what to do. He went to his room, showered, and changed clothes. If he was going to have a showdown with Nancy at least he could look a little more formal than the dungarees he'd worn to the picnic.

He took a fast shower and changed into a fresh pair of pants with a matching golf shirt. Downstairs, Mrs. Doyle met him.

"You're going out, sir?" Her face was curious because normally when Sam came home, he stayed home.

"Yes, I have some business to resolve. I'll let the Officer of the Deck know I'll be off base for a few hours."

Sam left the base and drove to Nancy's not even bothering to telephone her to make sure she was home. If David was spending the weekend, there was a good chance she'd be there.

There were lights on in the house when he pulled in the driveway. He parked his car and got out into the cool night. When he pushed the bell, he heard the chimes ringing. After a while, he heard footsteps stop at the door.

* * * *

"Who's there?" Nancy said as she looked out the peephole.

"It's me, Sam." His fists were clenched by his sides.

She opened the door and quickly pulled him inside. "Sam, what the devil are you doing, coming here at this time of night?" Her exasperation showed as he pushed past her into the den.

"Is David here?"

"No, he's spending the night at Mac's house with the boys."

"Good, we have to talk."

Her heart froze with fear. The way he was acting showed he was upset. One look at his face and she knew why he had come. She tried not to let her nervousness show.

"Did you like the miniature swan David brought you for your birthday?" he demanded.

"How did you know about his gift?" A cold chill ran down her spine. She hadn't wanted him to find out about David this way.

"Beth and I were at the exchange when he brought it for you, and he mentioned his father always said his mother looked like an 'elegant swan.' He could have only heard it from you."

Nancy looked at him dumbfounded. "You were there? The color left her face as she sank into a nearby chair.

"He said he had his eye on it for some time and wanted to buy it for your birthday."

Her whole world collapsed. Confused, she struggled to regain control.

"David is my son, isn't he? I went back to the office and checked out your file."

"Yes, he's your son. Did you think I would deny it?"

"Why didn't you tell me?"

"Damn it, I wrote and told you. What was I suppose to do? Go up to you and say, oh, by the way Captain, remember that affair we had a long time ago, you went off to war and left me pregnant.

"We're back to the letters, I told you I never received any mail from you. Do you know what it's like to see other men getting mail but not you?" His anger showed.

"I can imagine, but I wrote. I was so happy when I learned I was pregnant, and I thought you'd be happy too. I never heard from you. I think Rita had something to do with us not receiving each other's mail."

"Why would your sister do something like that?"

"She's jealous. She always took the mail to the box and picked it up. I've tried to talk to her, but we always seem to miss each other. She's deliberately avoiding me."

"Mac said you were one of the best officers he has. Did you resign your commission because of me?"

"Isn't it obvious? The father of my son is my new commanding officer. Don't you think that alone would cause an unwanted situation?"

"I already told you I'm not getting married."

"It doesn't matter. You'll be rid of me in a few weeks."

"What makes you think I want to be rid of you?"

"Don't you?" Her heart did flip-flops. Surprised at his words, she stared at him.

"Yes, but not in the way you think. Getting rid of the uniform makes it a whole new ball game, my Elegant Swan."

Nancy couldn't believe what she heard. Her toes curled up and her heart pounded so loud she thought Sam would hear it. She wanted to believe him, but she wasn't about to give her heart away to a few encouraging words.

Before she could say anything, he continued. "I want to talk about David."

"What about David? He's mine. I'm the one who cared for him and loved him when his father didn't want him."

"How can you say that when I didn't know about him," Sam said, running his hand through his hair.

"Would it have mattered if you had known about him?"

"Damn right, it would have. Does he know anything about me?" he demanded.

"He knows some things about you, but I haven't told him you're here or that you're his father. Damn it, Sam, you walk in and out of my life like a revolving door and expect me to bow to your wishes. For the sake of both of us, I think it would be better if we wait to discuss this matter until after I get out. Then we can sit down and discuss it in a rational manner. We're both upset now, and I think it would be a good idea for you to leave."

"And if I disagree," His stubbornness showed.

"You'll agree, because you know it's the best thing for both of us. I don't think you want to end your naval career right now. It's bad enough you came here. If someone sees and recognizes you, you'd have a lot of explaining to do."

Neither of them was in a reasonable mood when it came to discussing David. Sam knew there was one thing he was going to do before he left. He didn't give Nancy a chance to move away before he pulled her into his arms and gave her a kiss that rocked her right down to her toes.

Chapter Twenty-four

After Sam left, Nancy remained on edge. She had a hard time getting to sleep. Thinking about his words and then the way he kissed her sent more than sensations of want reeling through her body.

He had been as adamant about writing to her as she had been. What reason would Rita or anyone have for taking their mail? Just to be spiteful and hurt her. To keep Sam away from her and his son was more than vengeful. The more Nancy considered it, the more inclined she was to believe it was Rita who sabotaged their romance. She didn't like thinking that about her sister, but hatred and jealousy were Rita's good friends. Sometimes Nancy thought she had her sister figured out, but when she learned the truth, she gave up trying.

Finally dozing off, Nancy woke with a start. Her sister's smug countenance flashed before her. Rita had wanted Sam, all the time, even though she claimed she didn't. Sam had turned away from her before he learned what she was really like.

Remembering that night at the club and Rita's rage, she should have known better than to believe anything her sister said, especially about not wanting Sam.

When Rita learned Nancy was pregnant with Sam's baby, she went into a slump. She called Nancy all kinds of names. Dad had put an instant stop to that and threatened to put Rita back in the hospital. She'd have thought nothing of taking their letters and breaking up their romance. She'd see it as a way at getting even with both of them.

Nancy didn't believe Rita would have done such a thing on her own. Tom must have put the idea in her head. Living in the cottage at the end of the lane near the mailbox gave her ample opportunity to do so, and no one would be the wiser. Rita still loved Tom then. Maybe she had done it for him, hoping he would return her love. Remembering her father's words about Rita and liquor, Nancy suspected Tom was probably the one who supplied the liquor.

Nancy got out of bed and went into the kitchen. She made tea and took it out to the terrace. The cool night would clear her head.

She sat there for hours mulling over her thoughts. If the problem had been the U.S. mail, some letters would have made it through. No one had thought of Rita at the time. What better way for her to pick up the mail and keep the ones sent from Sam. The ones Rita knew Nancy wanted. If Rita was caught, she would lie and deny it. She must have them hidden somewhere. To confront her was the only way to know for sure if she kept any of the letters. Rita had accomplished what she wanted by separating Sam and Nancy.

When David was born, Rita had disliked him because he was Sam's son and very much like him. Nancy pitied her. How Rita hated being pitied.

Next weekend she'd make sure to see Rita and have it out with her. She wrapped her robe around tighter against the early morning dawn and slept, trusting she had found the answer to the missing letters.

Chapter Twenty-five

For Nancy, the week began with a bang. A lot of Thursty's work ended in Nancy's lap. She didn't really mind, because it kept her busy and her mind off Sam.

The week finally passed. Friday, her phone rang. "Lieutenant Smith-Owens."

"Hi, it's me," Mike said. "Am I interrupting anything?"

"Not anything important. No one's here except Lieutenant Thurston and me. What's up? I haven't heard or seen you in ages."

"I know, I've been busy," he said sheepishly.

"With Trina?" She could tell he was excited.

"Yeah, how did you know?"

She smiled into the phone. "It was just a good guess. How's it going?" She wasn't going to tell him she'd heard the rumors that he was seeing Trina.

"I'm changing my spots."

"Oh? In what way?" Curiosity was getting the better of her. A small stab of emptiness invaded her heart.

"I've asked Trina to marry me, but..." The happiness in his voice danced over the wires.

"Oh Mike, that's wonderful. She said yes, of course."

"She sure did. It took some persuading, but I did it. You're not upset with me for not telling you sooner."

"Why should I be?" She was glad Mike finally realized he loved Trina.

"When's the big affair?"

"Not for a while. I want to give Trina time to get used to the idea, and it'll give me time to get to know the kids."

"That's playing it smart. I'm very happy for you."

"Are you staying in town this weekend?"

"No, I'm going home. I have some business to resolve."

"Meet us at the club for a drink before you go, and we'll tell you all about it."

"I can't stay long."

"Trina and I just want to talk to you."

"Okay, I'll meet you at the club after work around five-thirty."

"See you then."

Nancy hung up the phone, cleared her desk for the weekend and left.

On Friday afternoon the club was always crowded. Everyone was having drinks before heading home or out of town. Nancy found Mike at the bar with Trina. She reached over and hugged Trina.

"I hear congratulations are in order for you and Mike."

"Thanks." Trina was all smiles for the first time in a long while.

"Trina thought you'd be upset with us not telling you right away."

The bartender set a glass of tonic water and lime in front of her. Nancy was surprised to have it arrive so fast.

"Don't look so surprised, Nancy. Mike ordered it when he saw you by the door," Trina said.

"Thank you, Mike. Best wishes and many happy years ahead for you both." They raised their glasses in unison.

"Thanks, hon." Mike reached over and kissed Nancy on the cheek.

"Hey watch that stuff in public." Trina grinned at them.

"You won't have to worry about Mike," Nancy said. "He's a straight shooter."

She took another swallow of her drink and put her glass down. "I hate to be a spoil sport, but I have to run. Keep in touch and let me know when the big event is?"

"You'll be the first to know," Trina replied.

Nancy buzzed them both on the cheek and left. She drove to her sister's house, hoping the rest of the evening would go as well as the beginning had.

Chapter Twenty-six

Later that night, when Nancy turned in the lane by the cottage, every light in the house burned bright. Rita always kept the lights going full blast with no regard to the cost.

Nancy pulled in the front drive and parked. Now was as good a time as any to talk to Rita and clear up this mess. She rang the bell several times before Rita answered.

Her sister swung the door wide so it hit the wall with a thud. Nancy took in her disheveled appearance—smeared makeup, whiskey on her breath, and her hair lank and dirty around her face. Her shirt and slacks were ripped, buttoned wrong, and food stained. In her good days, her sister had always been a neat freak in everything. Nancy had never seen her sister ever look this bad.

"Oh, it's you, Miss Goodie-two-shoes." Rita started to pull the door back and slam it in Nancy's face. Nancy pushed her hand up to stop it.

"I don't have any anything to discuss with you." Scorn filled Rita's voice.

"The letters," Nancy spat out the words. She grabbed her sister's arm and held it. This time she wasn't going to let her slip away.

A look of fright replaced Rita's smug look. "What letters?"

"You know what letters."

"I have no idea what you're talking about."

"You know damn well what I'm talking about. The letters I wrote to Sam and the letters he wrote to me. You stole them."

"Oh, those letters. They're around here somewhere. Anyway, he didn't write them to you. He wrote them to me. He was in love with me and asked me to marry him. We were going to have a baby."

Nancy stared at her sister in disbelief. She had really flipped this time.

"You're lying. It's all in your sick mind. Sam was never in love with you. You were so jealous of my having Sam's baby, you decided to punish us by taking our letters. You couldn't stand David because each day he became more and more like Sam. You stopped David from knowing his father, and you didn't give a damn about me, especially if you could find another way to hurt me."

"I did, didn't I? Shut up, Miss Prim-and-Proper. I don't want to talk to you anymore." Rita turned her back on her.

Nancy wasn't the easygoing sister anymore. She had a good grip on Rita and swung her back around.

"Ouch, that hurt," she shouted at Nancy. "I have nothing to say to you."

"I think you do. You didn't expect me to find out about the letters, did you?"

"It wasn't my idea."

"It was Tom's idea, wasn't it? You'd do anything for him, hoping he'd return your love, or was it the whiskey?"

"Tom didn't want Sam to have you," Rita whimpered.

"Sam is here now and knows about David."

"He can't be here." She sounded surprised.

"Oh, but Sam is. He's my new commanding officer."

Rita pulled away from Nancy and stumbled, regained her balance, and stood in front of Nancy. She started to laugh, a throaty, hysterical laugh.

"You're in the Navy so you can't touch Sam and I can."

Nancy watched her sister and knew what she was going to say would push her deeper into madness. "I've got news for you, dear sister. I've resigned my commission, and I'll be a civilian in a few weeks. Then nothing can stop us. Sam still loves me."

"You can't have him. He's mine."

"Only in your mind. Sam never loved you, and Tom only wants you to do his dirty work. All these years you've been in love with Tom, he never returned that love. You thought by doing what he wanted, he would eventually turn to you. He never has, and now he loves someone else. Sam never was yours."

Nancy looked past Rita. "Where's your night nurse? Someone is supposed to be here with you at all times." She had been so upset with Rita, she hadn't thought about the nurses.

"He's here, somewhere." Rita started to laugh.

"Where?" Nancy demanded.

"In the kitchen."

Nancy went to look for the nurse and found him on the floor just coming to and rubbing the back of his head. He looked at Nancy blurry eyed. She helped him up.

"That sister of yours is a sneaky one. She lured me in here and whacked me with a frying pan."

Rita staggered into the kitchen carrying an empty bottle of whiskey. She tried to take a swig from it and swore. "Damn it, the bottle's empty."

Nancy ducked as her sister threw the bottle, and it smashed against the wall.

"You're still mixing your pills with whisky. Does Tom bring you the whisky?"

"It's none of your damn business who I see and what I do."

"Don't you see what he's doing to you?"

"We're friends and friends help each other. He wouldn't hurt me."

"Tom hurts anyone who gets in his way. He doesn't love anyone but himself. You're a liability."

"You're a liar." Rita sounded less certain.

"You were there the night he was drunk and ran over Esther Pierce."

Eyes wide, Rita stared at her. "How … how do you know that?"

"That night you came home crying and told me what happened. Tom didn't bother to stop or help her, and she died."

"You can't tell what I told you." Rita sounded a little more sober.

"You needn't worry. Where is Mrs. Belk?" Nancy kept her eyes on her sister.

"Sleeping it off," Rita said smugly.

"What do you mean?"

"I added a little something to her tea."

"You did what?" Astonished, Nancy looked around the room.

Mrs. Belk stood bleary eyed by the kitchen door. "I forgot how cunning she was. It won't happen again."

Rita let out a string of words that couldn't be repeated.

Mrs. Belk shook her head. "I think you'd better leave, Mrs. Smith-Owens. It's been a rough night."

"My sister can't go 'til I say goodnight," Rita insisted.

Nancy sighed. Rita slapped her across the face. The sudden blow stunned Nancy.

Not stopping to think, she returned the slap. Rita looked dazed.

"My dear sister, Dad should have put you in a home long before this."

Rita crumpled to the floor in a fetal position whimpering and playing for sympathy. Nancy no longer had any for her.

* * * *

After the confrontation with her sister last weekend, Nancy was worn out with all the things happening in her life. In a few days she would be free of all military responsibilities. She was busy filing a BUPERS manpower report when her phone rang.

She dropped the report on her desk and answered the phone. "Lieutenant Smith---."

Her father's unsteady voice brought her to a sudden halt. Something was wrong. He never called her at work.

"What's wrong, Dad?"

"Darling, I'm sorry to bother you, but…"

"Dad, it's okay. What's wrong?" Her vice was urgent and demanding. A strange feeling came over as she waited. "What's wrong?"

"Rita's dead." His voice faltered.

"She's dead? How?" An overwhelming sadness hit her. "How did she die?"

"It happened sometime during the night. She fell down the stairs and broke her neck."

"Was she drunk?"

"Yes. The nurse found her this morning. The Emergency Medical Team said she died immediately and didn't suffer."

Her heart sank. The last time she saw Rita they had fought. Shivers ran down her spine.

"Nancy, are you still there?"

"Yes, I'm still here. It's just a shock. How's Joe taking it?"

"Not good, even though he and Rita were separated. He's making all the funeral arrangements. The funeral will probably be on Friday at Saint Luke's Cemetery. It is just going to be a graveside service."

"You can tell me about it when I get home. You needn't worry. I'll be there. Let me know if anything changes."

"It's a shock to all of us and yet again…" Her father's voice cracked.

"I know it is. I'll be home as soon as I can."

"Thank you. I know you and your sister never saw eye to eye. Ruth and I really appreciate you coming."

The sadness in her father's voice hurt. "It will be Friday before I can get home, but, I'll be there."

"That's fine. The neighbors will be stopping in after the ceremony. Leona and Mattie offered to put in extra time. Just get here when you can. I love you."

"I will. I love you too."

Nancy hung up the phone and turned to see Thursty at her desk pretending to work. She had heard all of Nancy's conversation with her father. Holding back the tears, Nancy sat down at her desk as she heard Thursty approach.

"Something bad has happened. Want to talk about it?" She stood by Nancy's desk waiting for her to answer.

"My sister fell down a flight of stairs and broke her neck. She died instantly." Nancy choked on the words, but was able to get them out.

"I'm sorry to hear that. Is there anything I can do?"

Thursty very seldom offered to help anyone, and it caught Nancy off guard.

"When is the funeral?"

"It's this Friday."

"If you need anything, just let me know. I'm sure you won't have any trouble getting off."

"No, I don't expect so. There isn't much going on right now. Thanks for your offer."

Nancy noticed the difference in Thursty. Something was softer and more caring about her. She had never been concerned or friendly before. It confirmed Nancy's feeling that she must have a lover. As they were talking, a yeoman approached them and handed Nancy a bouquet of flowers.

Nancy started to open the card and then saw it was addressed to Thursty, the handwriting looked familiar but she couldn't place it. "Thursty these are for you, not me." She handed the flowers to her.

"Who would be sending me flowers?" Thursty opened the card and a big smile crossed her face.

"It must be someone special."

"It is someone very special." Thursty looked happy. Nancy guessed she had a secret she didn't want to share.

That night Nancy called David and told him of his aunt's death. He was sad, but relieved when she told him he didn't have to come home for the service.

* * * *

When she arrived at the farm on Friday morning, friends and neighbors were already stopping by to drop off all kinds of food for after the service. In this part of the country, it was a tradition for everyone to come back to the house after the service. There was always plenty of food and drink waiting for the guests.

Nancy slipped in the kitchen door where Mattie and Leona were hard at work. "Good morning, ladies."

"Oh, honey, it's so good to see you," Mattie said. "You're a ray of sunshine on gloomy day."

Just then, her father entered the kitchen. "I thought I heard your car drive up."

"I didn't want to use the front door. There were so many cars parked in front."

"Smart girl. People have been coming and going, dropping off food." He set a cake on the table.

Putting his arms around her, he hugged her. Ruth had followed him. Her father let her go, and Ruth hugged her, too.

"I'm glad I could be here. I'll stay in the kitchen and help Mattie, if it's okay with you, Dad?"

"That will be fine," her father said, holding her hand and not wanting to let go. Her father and Ruth looked beat.

Mattie handed her an apron, and they set to work. "I'm sure glad you could get home, Miss Nancy."

"Mattie, you know it's always good to be home under any circumstances."

"You can cut up that nice pecan cake Mrs. Wolfe brought over and put it on this here plate. There's a roll of plastic on the table. Take a piece and cover it when you finish. Don't know why I'm telling yow how to do it when you already know how."

"It's all right, Mattie. We're all on edge." Nancy gave her a big smile.

She took the cake plate and did as Mattie said. She worked quietly with the two women and both seemed appreciative of her help. It gave her father and Ruth time to get ready for the graveside service.

Mattie and Leona were considered part of the family. She knew how unhappy were at the loss of her sister and could imagine what they were feeling. Leona was close to Rita in age.

They were sisters. Mattie was a widow and Leona was happily married. Before Joe had left, he had hired Leona and Mrs. Belk to stay with Rita as a companion and nurse. How Leona could stand Rita's mood swings was beyond Nancy's comprehension. She hoped Leona would tell her how her sister had died.

"Dad said Rita fell down the stairs and broke her neck," Nancy prompted.

"That she did," Leona confirmed. "It was a real nasty fall, as though she was reaching out to someone."

"She was alone at the time?"

"No, it was my night off, and Mrs. Belk thought Miss Rita had gone to bed and was sound asleep. Mrs. Belk was making herself some tea when she heard the scream and fall. She ran into the hallway and found Miss Rita at the foot of the stairs. She called nine-one-one right away and then me a few minutes later. The medics said she died of a broken neck. Mrs. Belk called you father and the ambulance arrived a few minutes later."

"The pills, the drinking, and the depression finally got to her this time," Nancy said.

"Yes." Leona sighed. "Mr. Joe's leaving didn't help. I can't say I blame him. He put up with an awful lot from your sister. He was building that nice big house on the point, and she didn't appreciate anything he did for her. A good man can just take so much. He did everything to please her, and she still wasn't satisfied. She finally drove him away."

"It's a wonder he didn't leave before," Nancy said.

"She was always carrying that box around," Leona said.

"What box?"

"What box? Did I say box, I meant the good book." Leona stopped talking. For some reason, Leona was trying to protect her sister.

Nancy decided to try another tack. "I understand Rita was drinking again. Where did the liquor come from?"

"I'm not sure, but the Senator came to see her a lot when he was in town. She'd be fine for a while and then slip right back into her depression. Miss Nancy, you know it isn't nice to speak ill of the dead."

Nancy had to stifle a smile. Hearing Tom brought the liquor didn't surprise her. She was still curious about the box.

"What kind of box did my sister carry around?"

Leona stared at Nancy for a moment. "It ... was a shoe box."

"That's big enough to hold letters, so where are they now?"

"Your father has them."

Nancy had a good idea of the box contents, but finding out would have to wait till later.

"Your sister took to reading the Bible before she died." Leona said quietly.

"The Bible?"

Rita reading the good book was absolutely absurd. Could it be possible she'd gotten religion? Was she looking for forgiveness and a way into heaven? Rita had to have a few good points.

Her father came into the kitchen carrying a large florist box and sent the maids away. He couldn't have timed his entrance any better. Now she wouldn't have to wait for any more answers. With everything going on it probably would be a few days before things settled down.

Her father handed her the florist box and cleared a place on the counter. "This is addressed to you."

In her heart, she knew they were from Sam before even opening the box. When she did, delicate pink roses, fern, and baby breath awaited her. A small white envelope was tied to one stem. Her father was curious as to who sent the flowers. She knew they weren't from the gang at the office because they had already sent a lovely spray of carnations for the funeral and Max and Stella had sent a sympathy bouquet to the house. She hadn't seen them, but had heard about them. They had been sent directly to the cemetery.

She was happy to see the flowers were from Sam. She handed the card to her father, and he read the words out loud .She looked at her father as tears streaked down her cheeks. He reached over with his handkerchief and wiped them away.

"That was very thoughtful of Sam."

"Yes, it was." She looked at her father. "Sam knows about David."

"You didn't tell him about David, and he found out another way."

"Yes, no, he found out accidentally."

"I doubt he was happy about that."

"He wasn't," she replied, half-smiling.

"I wouldn't be either." He looked at her, waiting for an explanation.

"Whose side are you on?" She smiled to take the sting out of her words.

He returned her smile. "Your side, of course."

"Actually it was a remark David made."

"Where did David meet Sam?"

"At the picnic. Afterwards, David wanted to go to the exchange to buy my birthday present. He told me he'd seen something special there and thought I would like it."

"What was it?" Her father looked curious.

"It was a small, cut glass swan."

"Did you like it?"

"Yes, very much. David remembered me telling him years ago about his father saying with my short dark hair and long neck I looked like an 'Elegant Swan.' Sam was there with his daughter Beth and overheard David's conversation with the sales clerk. It struck a cord with him." She paused a moment.

"Dad, David never told me about meeting them. We went to dinner that night, and he gave me the swan. It's beautiful. After dinner, I dropped David off at Mac's to spend the night with his boys. I came home to rest and relax only that didn't happen."

Nancy sighed before continuing. "About ten that night, Sam showed up at the beach house in a state. I was glad David wasn't there to hear us argue."

"Sam now knows he has a son. He's hurt you never let him know. You still haven't told David about his father."

"No. I only have a short time left in the navy. My discussion with Sam will have to wait until I'm out."

"He won't like that. I don't think I would either." His father stern face made his feelings clear.

"You're supposed to be my side," she said.

He didn't have a chance to answer as Ruth entered the room. "Joe is here, and it's time to go to the cemetery."

* * * *

Time had slipped by talking to her father about her personal problems. Nancy knew Tom would attend the service for Rita. Like all the other guests, he would come back to the house after the service.

He was still a friend of the family and of Joe, but today of all days, she didn't want to deal with him. She wondered if he would mention his offer, or wait until a more appropriate time. He wouldn't have to wait for her answer.

She had other things on her mind such as the letters and Holly House. The house was almost ready for the move. She had already listed her beach house with a realtor, and with the market the way it was, it would sell quickly.

Maybe her sister had found religion before she died and that's why Joe had opted for a short graveside service. Rita had lived all her life here and yet Nancy knew little about Rita's friends, or even if she had any. She hadn't been an easy person to know.

Nancy was surprised to see so many people at the ceremony. A lot of them came out of respect for her parents who were well liked in the town. She stood with Mattie and Leona slightly behind her father and

Ruth and shed tears with them for her sister. Lost in thought, she almost missed the minister's last words.

"May our dearly beloved Rita, rest in peace for all eternity. Amen."

'Amen' loud and clear echoed through the churchyard. The minister had ended the sermon. Nancy placed several red roses on her sister's casket. Despite all their quarrels, she still loved Rita even though there were times when she had hated her.

After the funeral, the more she thought about the letters, the more incensed she became. Would she ever know? The sickness had eaten away at her sister's brain and made her an irrational person. Rita's jealousy had centered on Nancy for Sam wanting her more than he wanted Rita. Damn, she had no idea Rita hated her that much. Even if they didn't get along, she would have never expected her to be so vindictive.

She couldn't deprive David from knowing his father and his half sister. The three of them would have to come to some agreement to satisfy all of them. Sharing David with people other than her immediate family would be hard to do, but she would do it for David.

The grounds keepers started lowering the casket into the grave. Friends and neighbors gathered around the family expressing their deepest sympathy and condolences.

Before the ceremony, the sun had hidden behind dark threatening clouds. Now it shone in all its glory and her heart lifted with joy. She felt as if all her troubles had disappeared and it was a new beginning.

Chapter Twenty-seven

Nancy wandered through the house greeting old friends and accepting their condolences. There was no one with whom she really wanted to talk. She tried not to think about the letters, wishing the guests would leave so she could talk to her father about Rita. In another half hour all the guests had departed except for Tom and his parents.

"Let me say goodbye to them, then we can sit down and relax," Ruth said.

Nancy had avoided Tom as much as she could, knowing what she knew. She had finally recalled why the handwriting on the card with Thursty's bouquet looked familiar. It was Tom's. If he and Thursty were having a hush-hush affair, it was fine with her. It meant he would leave her alone. Now was as good a time to tell him her answer about his job offer.

Tom approached her with a smile. "Have you been avoiding me?"

"Of course, I have. You're not going to like my answer to your job offer."

"By that you mean no." He looked disappointed.

I'm sorry, Tom, I've decided to take time off and spend it with David."

"When I heard you brought Holly House, I had a feeling you weren't interested."

"Under the circumstances, we both know it wouldn't work out."

"I'm sorry anyway," he said, taking her hand in his.

"Just because you witnessed a little scene between Sam and me doesn't mean he's back in my life. On the contrary, it's just the opposite, and he knows about David." She pulled her hand away.

"So, you finally got around to telling him."

The knowledge that Sam knew about David seemed to deflate him. His smile disappeared. She let him think what he wanted. It was none of his business.

"I don't suppose he was too happy to hear he had a son after all these years," Tom said. "I wouldn't be, especially if I was in a high profile position and supposed to set an example for the future of our military."

"What happened between us, happened a long time ago. The differences between you and Sam are your priorities."

"What do you mean by that?"

"Haven't you ever wondered why I never accepted your invitations to go out after the first few times and later when you proposed?"

"It was because of Sam," he muttered.

"A long time ago it was part of it. I was still young and idealistic thinking he would come back to me. Then I realized to love someone didn't mean you would always be together and have a happy ending."

"Isn't that what we all expect?"

"Yes, love and being loved is what life is all about. I hope you tell Thursty those three little words. In all the years I've known you, I never heard you say the word love. I can't sit back and watch things happen. I have to be there helping it happen. My priorities have changed.

"My time in the service is almost up. As for what Sam decides to do about David, I have no idea. Once he has time to think the problem over, I'm sure we will be able to work things out. With Sam knowing, you no longer have a hold over us." She didn't want to use the word blackmail.

"I wasn't doing that."

"Weren't you? Politics filled your life, and I would always be on the sidelines waiting for you to acknowledge my presence. I know Thursty will not stand by and let you push her aside. You've latched on to a tiger, and, if you don't know it by now, you soon will."

"Who the hell are you talking about?" he snapped.

"As far as family is concerned, for you, politics takes place before anything else. I didn't think you wanted to share your life with anyone until now."

"What do you mean now?" He looked flustered.

"Those were expensive roses you sent Thursty, but they came to me by mistake. The handwriting looked familiar. At first, I didn't recognize it, and then I remembered."

"Who's Thursty?"

The look on his face was one she had seen when they were younger and he tried to cover up something he'd done wrong. He was lying.

"I hardly know the woman." His face turned bright scarlet.

"Well, at least you're telling some of the truth. You know her lot better than you want to admit. A man doesn't send expensive roses to someone he hardly knows."

His shoulders sagged. "How did you know?"

"The flowers. The next time let the florist do the writing. For the first time in your life, you've bitten off more than you can chew. She's the type of woman you need, and she'll stand by you. Good-bye, Tom." Nancy turned and left the room leaving him standing there with his mouth open and nothing to say.

* * * *

A few old friends had lingered behind, but left when they saw Tom and his parent's leave.

She was getting a cup of coffee when her father came into the kitchen.

"I see Tom didn't stick around," he said.

"I doubt we'll be seeing much of him in the future."

"Oh?" He didn't sound the least bit surprised.

"I told him I wasn't interest in his job offer. I have more important things to do."

"David and Sam," he acknowledged.

Mattie came into the kitchen carrying a tray of glasses.

"Mrs. Ruth is in the driveway saying good-by to the Senator and his folks," he said to the maid. "When she comes in, tell her Nancy and I will be in my study."

Nancy could tell something weighed heavily on her father's mind. She wondered what. Maybe it was something about the letters. He sat at his desk, and she sat in her favorite leather chair in front of him and waited.

"Truthfully, how is the situation between you and Sam?"

"I'm afraid the other night I wasn't being an obedient junior officer when I told him emphatically to hold off until I was a civilian. Then we could discuss our situation like normal people."

"I don't think that was a very good idea," her father said.

"I was furious with his attitude and just as upset as he was. Then he kissed me and rocked me right down to the soles of my shoes."

"And?"

"He turned around and left, leaving me standing there in a daze and wanting more. Damn him, why did I have to fall in love with a stubborn man like him."

She looked at her father and saw him smiling. "Okay I'll admit it, I'm still in love with him."

"I see," her father said. "I guess I shouldn't keep you in suspense any longer."

He reached down in the right hand drawer, brought out a shoebox, and set it on top of his desk. Removing the cover, he brought out a pack of letters from the box.

"My letters? I just found out Rita had taken them." She started to reach for them when her father stopped her.

"Before I give them to you, I want to tell you how they were found. You know your sister fell down the stairs and broke her neck. She was carrying this box of letters. It split open and the contents scattered all over the floor. Mrs. Belk quickly gathered them up before the EMTS and the police arrived. She believed them to be personal and brought them to me. Knowing it was nobody's business but the family's, there is an old saying. 'What people don't know, won't hurt them.' These are your letters to Sam and his letters to you."

Nancy now had proof her sister had stolen her letters, but it wasn't going to do her any good if Sam didn't come around.

"These belong to you," he said as he handed the letters to her.

She was not surprised to see they were well worn. Rita must have read them many times. She had ruined three lives with her jealousy. Maybe in time, she could forgive her sister.

She took her letters and got up to leave the room, when her father spoke. "I'll see Sam gets his letters and explain to him how they were found."

"I don't know if it matters now."

Sam had kissed her, but she wasn't sure he meant it.

* * * *

Outside, sitting on the swing, she laid the letters beside her. She took one from the ribbon tied packet and started to read.

To my 'Elegant Swan':

I've been assigned to go ashore with some of the patrols. It's a living hell out here in the jungle.

The day patrols are bad enough, but the night patrols are tough. You never know what's going to happen and the least bit of shadow and movement could mean the enemy and our eminent death. Sometime it's harder to tell our own men form the Vietnamese. I don't know what is worse, the heat and the humidity, or the snakes and other creepy crawlers. The place is covered with them. I have been many places in my life, but this is the worst. I miss you terribly. Just knowing you will be waiting for me gets me through the worst days and nights. I'll write when I can.

Love, Sam.

She skipped some of the gruesome parts and read only the parts where he said he loved and missed her. Sam's loneliness and his love came through in every one of his letters. He asked her to marry him and told her how much he loved her.

No wonder he had been devastated, thinking she didn't love him. Nancy didn't know how long she sat there reading his letters of love and their future to gather. Twilight had set in by the time she returned to the house.

Chapter Twenty-eight

Nancy was curious as to know how her father planned to approach Sam about the letters, and if he had already done so. He hadn't mentioned it to her, and, in a way, she was afraid to ask. She didn't want to know how Sam reacted, and yet she needed to know. All kinds of thoughts ran through her mind as to what Sam would do and when. It had been a month since she left the service, and still she hadn't heard from him.

Talking to Mac's wife Stella a few times, she learned they were busy with the upcoming quarterly inspection, and that Sam was attending a conference in Washington.

Nancy had turned over the beach house to the new owners who wanted the furniture with the house. It saved her from storing it because it wouldn't fit in Holly House, the colonial house she now owned. The things she wanted to keep, she had shipped with a local mover. She had packed her personal things and brought them with her.

Leona was waiting for her when she arrived. She had offered her services to help until Nancy settled in. Nancy had gratefully accepted her offer. It was nice, and she was never in the way.

For the first few weeks, Nancy slept in with no rules and regulations to follow. For now, she missed them, but knew it wouldn't be long before they were forgotten. The old routine gave way to the new. It was strange at first, but she was looking forward to being a mother and being home for David.

She thought of Sam and the months they lived together. It would be nice to be here and welcome him home. She hoped he didn't blame her too much. Her letters proved she had written and that she loved him. She had hoped she would have heard from him by now.

Sam had told Mac about them, and, of course, he told Stella. In one of her phone calls, Stella mentioned Sam was showing up at the social affair alone. Dared she hope?

Nancy hired a local gardener to cut back the holly bushes, clean the flowerbeds, and paint the outside. The brickwork also needed cleaning, but it could wait until later. The gutters and the roof had already been inspected and were all right.

Her protection was Rebel, David's new German Sheppard puppy that slept on the floor at the bottom of her bed when David wasn't home. When David came home, Rebel sprawled across the foot of his bed. At times, the dog seemed more friendly and human than some of the people she had met in her life.

Leona helped her place her crystal in the old china cabinet she had inherited from the former owner. "It's mighty nice you want to use this fine china cabinet Mrs. Jeffery left behind." Leona beamed with pride.

"The pieces she left are very nice. It's too bad she had no one to inherit them," Nancy said.

Nancy had carefully packed the crystal swan and carried it home, not wanting to a take a chance it would get broken. She was placing in on the top shelf when the telephone rang, shattering the afternoon silence.

She started to answer 'Lieutenant Smith-Owens' when she caught herself. "This is Mrs. Smith-Owens."

"Mrs. Smith-Owens, I'm so glad I found you at home. This is Superintendent Grayson at Clairemont Military Academy."

Nancy panicked. Something was wrong. "What is it? Has something happened to David?"

"I'm afraid so. One of the school vans in which he was riding was broadsided by a truck that went through a red light."

"Oh, Dear God, how bad was he hurt? Is he all right?" All kinds of horrible thoughts ran through her mind. She finally got a grip on herself.

"We don't know. The students were rushed immediately to Clairemont General about ten miles from here. David seems to be the most seriously hurt."

"How bad?"

"What we know so far is he has a broken right leg and some internal injuries."

"I'll be there as soon as I can." It didn't sound good. She didn't wait to hear anymore and dialed her father.

"Hello, Smith residence."

Nancy cut her father off before he could finish, "David's been hurt in an accident. I have to go to him." Anxiety filled her voice.

"I'll go with you. You sound too upset to drive."

"Great, I wasn't looking forward to the long drive." After talking to her father, she made a quick call to Mac.

"This is Commander MacLane's office."

"Mac, thank goodness I caught you. It's Nancy, I need to get in touch with Sam. I know he's away, but David's been hurt in an accident at school. I thought he should know."

"How bad is it?"

"All I know is he has a broken leg and some internal injuries."

"I'll get in touch with the Captain right away."

She heard the urgency in Mac's voice. "David's at Clairemont General Hospital in Clairemont. I've got to run. Dad's here. He's going to drive."

"I'll get in touch with Sam, and be careful."

"Thanks, Mac." She hung up the phone.

It was a good thing her father offered to drive. She was a wreck from worrying. She grabbed her handbag and a jacket. It would be cool in the mountains. She prayed nothing would happen to David before he got to know his father and that his internal injures were not serious. The four-hour drive dragged past. Yet she could remember nothing about it.

Darkness set in by the time they reached Clairemont General. It was an old three-story building right out of Virginia's past, dating back to the eighteen hundreds. Inside, they encountered the usual hustle and bustle found in most hospitals.

Mr. Grayson came to meet her. "I'm so glad you could come." He still had a strong, firm body from his years in the service.

"Do you remember my father?"

Mr. Grayson offered his hand to her father. "It's good to see you again, Mr. Smith. I'm sorry it has to be under these circumstances."

"So am I," Edward replied. He shook the hand Grayson offered.

"How is he?" Nancy said.

"He's still in surgery. The doctor confirmed he had a broken leg and some minor internal injuries."

"When do you think we can see him?"

"Once the doctor thinks it's advisable. Your David and Larry Thompson were hurt the worst. Please, come and sit down. Would you like some coffee?"

"No, thank you, I'm nervous enough and coffee will only make me more so."

Grayson looked at her father.

"None for me, thank you."

Grayson led them to a private waiting room where they sat down in comfortable chairs to wait.

"I hope you don't mind if I leave. I have some other business to attend to," Grayson said. "You can wait here. I'll inform the nurse you've arrived."

"Thank you," Edward answered for both of them. "This will be fine."

The time dragged past and the waiting became monotonous. Some people spoke in whispers and went away. A good two hours passed before a doctor came to talk with them.

"Mrs. Smith-Owens?"

"I'm Mrs. Smith Owens." She was getting used to being call Mrs. Smith-Owens instead of Lieutenant.

The doctor was tall, lean, and looked tired. "You son has a fractured leg and some internal injuries. At first we though his leg was broken in two places, but, on further examination, we only found one fracture and some badly bruised muscles. The internal injuries he has are minor. He also has a badly bruised shoulder and a broken right wrist and a few lacerations. It will take about eight weeks for his breaks to heal. He has some cuts from the flying glass. They should heal easily, and there was no glass embed in his cheeks. He's a very lucky young man."

"Thank goodness it isn't worse." Nancy released a big sigh.

"He's in recovery, and it will be awhile before you can see him.

He's still feeling the affects of the anesthesia and is semi-conscious, but it should wear off in a few hours. He's not remembering the accident right now, but I'm hoping that will only be temporary. The loss of memory is probably caused by the trauma form the accident."

"When can I see him?"

"You can see him for a few moments. He'll be groggy and probably not know you're here. He's a strong young man, and he'll be roaring to get back on his feet. The nurse will inform you when you can see him. His prognosis is excellent. You needn't worry."

Before they could thank him, he was paged and left the room. The nurse came by about an hour later.

"Mrs. Smith-Owens, if you'll come this way I'll take you to your son's room. You may see him for a few minutes."

"You go," her father said. "I'll wait here."

When she entered the room, she quailed at the sight of David under all those machines that monitored his vital signs. A cast just above his knee covered his right leg, and he had two bandages on his face. At least the damage was on his left side instead of his good side.

She sat in a chair and held David's hand. She watched him breathe, all the monitors quietly doing their job. He appeared so small and pale. Tears filled her eyes.

The long hours slipped from night to day and day into night again. On the third day, Nancy slumped, thoroughly exhausted in a chair with her head resting on David's bed.

She woke to Sam gently shaking her. "Nancy, wake up, darling."

"Sam?" Half-asleep and half-awake, she peered up at him.

"I'm sorry not to be here sooner. I had to do some fast-talking to the Admiral. He wanted to know where I had acquired a son on such short notice. Fortunately, your father had given me your letters and enclosed a copy of David's birth certificate."

Nancy stared, trying to orient herself and absorb what Sam said. He pulled her up from the chair and into his arms. It felt so good being there. She hadn't felt this good in years. The missing years didn't matter nay more. She was half-smiling and half-crying.

"Oh God, it's so good to be in your arms again, Sam." Nancy thought he was going to squeeze the breath out of her.

"You're right where you belong, my love."

He kissed her again, and they were lost in their own little world. Wide-awake now, she realized there was someone standing next to him pulling on his shirt.

Beth looked at her with a big smile on her face. "Hi, remember me? I'm Beth."

"Of course, I remember you." Nancy returned Beth's smile. "How could I forget such a charming young lady?"

The little girl blushed and hid behind her father. Nancy looked at Sam for guidance.

"She knows and insisted on coming along to see David. It seems she's taken a liking to him. I explained to her about us on the way here."

"Beth, I'm sure David will be glad to see you." A discreet cough from her father caught her attention.

"I made reservations at the hotel across the street. Why don't we go there and get something to eat and some much needed rest now we know David is going to be all right."

Nancy had only catnapped the last couple of days and started to protest, but, Sam spoke. "That's a great idea. We all could use some sleep."

"What about David?" Nancy's maternal instincts rose.

"We can leave a message at the desk as to where we are," her father told her. "If there are any changes, they'll call us."

"I want to stay here," Nancy said with a sullen face.

"No. We're all exhausted and need to rest. I 'm sure David wouldn't want to see us disheveled, tired, and upset."

Sam put his arm around Nancy and herded her toward the door and to their cars in the parking lot. At the hotel, she was so tired she paid no attention to the people and things around her. All she knew was the bed felt good and was asleep in no time with Sam's arms around her and Beth asleep in the other bed.

When she woke, she had no idea how long she had slept, but felt much better. She looked across the room and saw Sam reading to Beth. The clock on the nightstand said four-thirty in the afternoon. She had slept all day.

"Good afternoon, sleepy head," Sam teased.

"Oh, Sam, you shouldn't have let me sleep so long. Did you and Beth get some sleep?"

"Yes, so did your father. He's in the room across the hall. David's doing fine. The doctor is pleased with his progress. He's been awake and complaining he's hungry."

"I don't know what I would do if anything happened to him."

Sam got up and came over to her. He took her hand in his and pulled her up from the bed and into his arms. He was wearing a sport shirt and slacks. Nancy still wore the same clothes she had come in a few days ago.

"Darling, nothing is going to happen to our son. He's strong, and if he's anything like his mother, he'll look back on this as a part of growing up."

"I want to see him now. Let me wash up."

"All right, but first there's something we have to talk about."

"Can't it wait?" Nancy recognized the determined sound in his voice.

"No, it can't." He sounded like a commanding officer.

"What is so important it can't wait?"

"I've put my papers in to retire."

"You did what?" His words stunned her.

"You heard me loud and clear," he said with a smile on his face.

"But why would you do that?" All kinds of reasons ran through her mind.

"About a month ago your father gave me your letters and told me what Rita had done. Your sister's jealousy and unhappiness kept us apart. I've missed all those years of being a part of your life and David's. I want to marry you and spend the rest of my life making it up to both of you."

"Oh, Sam, you have such a bright future and worked so hard to get where you are."

He kissed her. "I've devoted thirty years to the Navy. Now I intend to devote the next thirty years and more to my wife and family."

She kissed him again, looking happy for once. "I want to go and see David. Let's talk later."

"All right."

When they reached David's room, the nurse informed them David was alert and grumbling that he was hungry.

"That's our son." Nancy used the word 'our' instead 'my' knowing it would make Sam happy.

She looked at her battered and bruised son and ran to his bed. She put her arms gently around him.

"Mom, don't squeeze too hard. I'm sore all over."

"I'm sorry, darling." She pulled back.

"Hi, Dad." David's words came out loud and clear. Nancy looked at her son in surprise.

"Hi, son." Sam's smile could light up a whole city. He beamed with joy and shook David's good hand.

A tug on Sam's shirt drew his attention, and Beth moved forward.

"Hi, Squirt." David said in a voice not quite his own.

Beth smiled at him, grabbing his hand. Before anyone could move, she was climbing up on the side of his bed, and, in low voices, the two of them carried on a conversation, ignoring the grown ups. Sam and Nancy looked at each other thunderstruck by the rapport between the two children.

"David, how long have you known Sam was your father?"

"I figured it out the day of the picnic. He asked me about my bracelet when it fell off. He picked it up and must have seen the words on the other side. He had a strange look on his face. At the exchange he acted like he's been shot in the gut when I mentioned my father always said my mother looked like an elegant swan."

"You didn't mention meeting Sam in the exchange."

"I thought it better not to. You were upset enough."

"Oh you did, did you?" Nancy grinned at him.

"You didn't start getting nervous and upset until he arrived. One day you asked me to get something off your bureau, and I noticed the bottom drawer ajar. I wasn't really snooping. The drawer hadn't closed properly and, when I tried to close it, my curiosity got the better of me and then I saw the pictures. I figured there had been something between the two of you a long time ago." He watched to see how his parents reacted to his knowing.

"Oh, David, you're so right. Your Dad and I go back a long way."

Nancy smiled at him .He seemed to be coming through his ordeal with high spirits.

"We're glad your feeling better, son," Sam said. Can we get you anything?"

"I have everything I need but one thing. Get married and make us a family."

The End

About the Author
June Bradley

June E. Bradley started writing in her late teens after seeing Daphne DeMuir's, 'Rebecca.' It reminded her of the many stately Mansions she saw every weekend in Newport Rhode Island.

Her family would often drive along Ocean Drive, and admire all the beautiful homes. She often wondered what secrets laid behind those tall stone walls and iron gates. Newport and the Navy still have a special place in her heart and influence her writing. Her husband retired after thirty years and she still misses that way of life.

After a long illness then the death of her husband she started writing again. June has two grown children, four grandchildren and resides in Chesapeake, VA.

She has one book published by Hardshell Word Factory through Mundania Press, called 'Shannon's Creek' which is a Paranormal Romantic.

.

www.ingramcontent.com/pod-product-compliance
Lightning Source LLC
Chambersburg PA
CBHW032204190626
46810CB00018B/1426